Alfred Tennyson

Ballads and other Poems

Alfred Tennyson

Ballads and other Poems

ISBN/EAN: 9783743306189

Manufactured in Europe, USA, Canada, Australia, Japa

Cover: Foto ©Andreas Hilbeck / pixelio.de

Manufactured and distributed by brebook publishing software
(www.brebook.com)

Alfred Tennyson

Ballads and other Poems

LONDON

KEGAN PAUL & CO., 1 PATERNOSTER SQUARE

1880

TO

ALFRED TENNYSON

MY GRANDSON

Golden-hair'd Ally whose name is one with mine,

Crazy with laughter and babble and earth's new wine,

Now that the flower of a year and a half is thine,

O little blossom, O mine, and mine of mine,

Glorious poet who never hast written a line,

Laugh, for the name at the head of my verse is thine.

May'st thou never be wrong'd by the name that is mine!

CONTENTS.

———◦◦◦———

BALLADS AND OTHER POEMS.

THE FIRST QUARREL.

I.

'WAIT a little,' you say, 'you are sure it 'll all come
  right,'

But the boy was born i' trouble, an' looks so wan an'
  so white :

Wait! an' once I ha' waited—I hadn't to wait for long.

Now I wait, wait, wait for Harry.—No, no, you are
  doing me wrong!

Harry and I were married : the boy can hold up his
  head,

The boy was born in wedlock, but after my man was
  dead ;

I ha' work'd for him fifteen years, an' I work an' I
wait to the end.

I am all alone in the world, an' you are my only friend.

II.

Doctor, if *you* can wait, I'll tell you the tale o' my
life.

When Harry an' I were children, he call'd me his own
little wife;

I was happy when I was with him, an' sorry when he
was away,

An' when we play'd together, I loved him better than
play;

He workt me the daisy chain—he made me the cowslip ball,

He fought the boys that were rude an' I loved him
better than all.

'assionate girl tho' I was, an' often at home in dis-

    grace,

never could quarrel with Harry—I had but to look

    in his face.

III.

'here was a farmer in Dorset of Harry's kin, that

    had need

)f a good stout lad at his farm; he sent, an' the

    father agreed;

o Harry was bound to the Dorsetshire farm for years

    an' for years;

walked with him down to the quay, poor lad, an'

    we parted in tears.

'he boat was beginning to move, we heard them

    a-ringing the bell,

I'll never love any but you, God bless you, my own

    little Nell.'

IV.

I was a child, an' he was a child, an' he came to harm ;

There was a girl, a hussy, that workt with him up at
the farm,

One had deceived her an' left her alone with her sin
an' her shame,

And so she was wicked with Harry; the girl was
the most to blame.

V.

And years went over till I that was little had grown
so tall,

The men would say of the maids ' Our Nelly's the
flower of 'em all.'

I didn't take heed o' *them*, but I taught myself all I
could

To make a good wife for Harry, when Harry came
home for good.

VI.

Often I seem'd unhappy, and often as happy too,

For I heard it abroad in the fields 'I'll never love any

but you ;'

'I'll never love any but you' the morning song of the

lark,

'I'll never love any but you' the nightingale's hymn

in the dark.

VII.

And Harry came home at last, but he look'd at me

sidelong and shy,

Vext me a bit, till he told me that so many years had

gone by,

I had grown so handsome and tall—that I might ha'

forgot him somehow—

For he thought—there were other lads—he was fear'd

to look at me now.

VIII.

Hard was the frost in the field, we were married o'
  Christmas day,

Married among the red berries, an' all as merry as
  May—

Those were the pleasant times, my house an' my man
  were my pride,

We seem'd like ships i' the Channel a-sailing with
  wind an' tide.

IX.

But work was scant in the Isle, tho' he tried the
  villages round,

So Harry went over the Solent to see if work could be
  found;

An' he wrote 'I ha' six weeks' work, little wife, so
  far as I know;

I'll come for an hour to-morrow, an' kiss you before I
  go.'

X.

So I set to righting the house, for wasn't he coming

that day ?

An' I hit on an old deal-box that was push'd in a

corner away,

It was full of old odds an' ends, an' a letter along wi'

the rest,

I had better ha' put my naked hand in a hornets' nest.

XI.

' Sweetheart '—this was the letter—this was the letter

I read—

' You promised to find me work near you, an' I wish

I was dead—

Didn't you kiss me an' promise ? you haven't done it,

my lad,

An' I almost died o' your going away, an' I wish that

I had.'

XII.

I too wish that I had—in the pleasant times that had
    past,

Before I quarrell'd with Harry—*my* quarrel—the first
    an' the last.

XIII.

For Harry came in, an' I flung him the letter that
    drove me wild,

An' he told it me all at once, as simple as any child,

'What can it matter, my lass, what I did wi' my
    single life ?

I ha' been as true to you as ever a man to his wife ;

An' *she* wasn't one o' the worst.' 'Then,' I said, 'I'm
    none o' the best.'

An' he smiled at me, 'Ain't you, my love ? Come,
    come, little wife, let it rest !

The man isn't like the woman, no need to make such
a stir.'

But he anger'd me all the more, an' I said 'You were
keeping with her,

When I was a-loving you all along an' the same as
before.'

An' he didn't speak for a while, an' he anger'd me
more and more.

Then he patted my hand in his gentle way, 'Let by-
gones be ! '

' Bygones ! you kept yours hush'd,' I said, ' when you
married me !

By-gones ma' be come-agains ; an' *she*—in her shame
an' her sin—

You'll have her to nurse my child, if I die o' my lying
in !

You'll make her its second mother ! I hate her—an'
I hate you !'

Ah, Harry, my man, you had better ha' beaten me
    black an' blue

Than ha' spoken as kind as you did, when I were so
    crazy wi' spite,

'Wait a little, my lass, I am sure it 'ill all come right.

XIV.

An' he took three turns in the rain, an' I watch'd him,
    an' when he came in

I felt that my heart was hard, he was all wet thro' to
    the skin,

An' I never said 'off wi' the wet,' I never said 'on
    wi' the dry,'

So I knew my heart was hard, when he came to bid
    me goodbye.

'You said that you hated me, Ellen, but that isn't
    true, you know;

I am going to leave you a bit—you'll kiss me before
    I go?'

XV.

'Going! you're going to her—kiss her—if you will,'
I said,—

I was near my time wi' the boy, I must ha' been light
i' my head—

'I had sooner be cursed than kiss'd!'—I didn't know
well what I meant,

But I turn'd my face from *him*, an' he turn'd *his* face
an' he went.

XVI.

And then he sent me a letter, 'I've gotten my work
to do;

You wouldn't kiss me, my lass, an' I never loved any
but you;

I am sorry for all the quarrel an' sorry for what she
wrote,

I ha' six weeks' work in Jersey an' go to-night by
the boat.'

XVII.

An' the wind began to rise, an' I thought of him out
at sea,

An' I felt I had been to blame; he was always kind
to me.

Wait a little, my lass, I am sure it 'ill all come
right '—

An' the boat went down that night—the boat went
down that night.

RIZPAH.

17—.

I.

WAILING, wailing, wailing, the wind over land and

sea—

And Willy's voice in the wind, ' O mother, come out

to me.'

Why should he call me to-night, when he knows that

I cannot go ?

For the downs are as bright as day, and the full moon

stares at the snow.

II.

We should be seen, my dear; they would spy us out
of the town.

The loud black nights for us, and the storm rushing
over the down,

When I cannot see my own hand, but am led by the
creak of the chain,

And grovel and grope for my son till I find myself
drenched with the rain.

III,

Anything fallen again? nay—what was there left to
fall?

I have taken them home, I have number'd the bones,
I have hidden them all.

What am I saying? and what are *you*? do you come
as a spy?

Falls? what falls? who knows? As the tree falls so
must it lie.

IV.

Who let her in ? how long has she been ? you—what
   have you heard ?

Why did you sit so quiet ? you never have spoken a
   word.

O—to pray with me—yes—a lady—none of their
   spies—

But the night has crept into my heart, and begun to
   darken my eyes.

V.

Ah—you, that have lived so soft, what should *you*
   know of the night,

The blast and the burning shame and the bitter frost
   and the fright ?

I have done it, while you were asleep—you were only
   made for the day.

I have gather'd my baby together—and now you may
   go your way.

VI.

Nay—for it's kind of you, Madam, to sit by an old
dying wife.

But say nothing hard of my boy, I have only an hour
of life.

I kiss'd my boy in the prison, before he went out to
die.

'They dared me to do it,' he said, and he never has
told me a lie.

I whipt him for robbing an orchard once when he was
but a child—

'The farmer dared me to do it,' he said; he was
always so wild—

And idle—and couldn't be idle—my Willy—he never
could rest.

The King should have made him a soldier, he would
have been one of his best.

VII.

But he lived with a lot of wild mates, and they never
would let him be good ;

They swore that he dare not rob the mail, and he
swore that he would ;

And he took no life, but he took one purse, and when
all was done

He flung it among his fellows—I'll none of it, said
my son.

VIII.

I came into court to the Judge and the lawyers. I
told them my tale,

God's own truth—but they kill'd him, they kill'd him
for robbing the mail.

c

They hang'd him in chains for a show—we had always

borne a good name—

To be hang'd for a thief—and then put away—isn't

that enough shame ?

Dust to dust—low down—let us hide ! but they set

him so high

That all the ships of the world could stare at him,

passing by.

God 'ill pardon the hell-black raven and horrible fowls

of the air,

But not the black heart of the lawyer who kill'd him

and hang'd him there.

IX.

And the jailer forced me away. I had bid him my

last goodbye ;

They had fasten'd the door of his cell. ' O mother ! '

I heard him cry.

I couldn't get back tho' I tried, he had something

further to say,

And now I never shall know it.   The jailer forced me

away.

X.

Then since I couldn't but hear that cry of my boy

that was dead,

They seized me and shut me up: they fasten'd me

down on my bed.

'Mother, O mother!'—he call'd in the dark to me

year after year—

They beat me for that, they beat me—you know that

I couldn't but hear;

And then at the last they found I had grown so stupid

and still

They let me abroad again—but the creatures had

worked their will.

XI.

Flesh of my flesh was gone, but bone of my bone was
> left—

I stole them all from the lawyers—and you, will you
> call it a theft ?—

My baby, the bones that had suck'd me, the bones
> that had laughed and had cried—

Theirs ? O no ! they are mine—not theirs—they had
> moved in my side.

XII.

Do you think I was scared by the bones ? I kiss'd
> 'em, I buried 'em all—

I can't dig deep, I am old—in the night by the
> churchyard wall.

My Willy 'ill rise up whole when the trumpet of
> judgment 'ill sound,

But I charge you never to say that I laid him in holy
> ground.

XIII.

They would scratch him up—they would hang him

again on the cursed tree.

Sin? O yes—we are sinners, I know—let all that be,

And read me a Bible verse of the Lord's good will

toward men—

' Full of compassion and mercy, the Lord '—let me

hear it again;

' Full of compassion and mercy—long-suffering.' Yes,

O yes!

For the lawyer is born but to murder—the Saviour

lives but to bless.

He'll never put on the black cap except for the worst

of the worst,

And the first may be last—I have heard it in church

—and the last may be first.

Suffering—O long-suffering—yes, as the Lord must
    know,

Year after year in the mist and the wind and the
    shower and the snow.

XIV.

Heard, have you? what? they have told you he never
    repented his sin.

How do they know it? are *they* his mother? are *you*
    of his kin?

Heard! have you ever heard, when the storm on the
    downs began,

The wind that 'ill wail like a child and the sea that
    'ill moan like a man?

XV.

Election, Election and Reprobation—it's all very well.

But I go to-night to my boy, and I shall not find him
    in Hell.

For I cared so much for my boy that the Lord has look'd into my care,

And He means me I'm sure to be happy with Willy, I know not where.

XVI.

And if *he* be lost—but to save *my* soul, that is all your desire:

Do you think that I care for *my* soul if my boy be gone to the fire?

I have been with God in the dark—go, go, you may leave me alone—

You never have borne a child—you are just as hard as a stone.

XVII.

Madam, I beg your pardon! I think that you mean to be kind,

But I cannot hear what you say for my Willy's voice in the wind—

The snow and the sky so bright—he used but to call
in the dark,

And he calls to me now from the church and not
from the gibbet—for hark !

Nay—you can hear it yourself—it is coming—shaking
the walls—

Willy—the moon's in a cloud——Good night.   I am
going.   He calls.

THE NORTHERN COBBLER.

I.

WAÏT till our Sally cooms in, fur thou mun a' sights[1]
  to tell.

Eh, but I be maäin glad to seeä tha sa 'arty an' well.

'Cast awaäy on a disolut land wi' a vartical soon[2]!'.

Strange fur to goä fur to think what saäilors a' seëan
  an' a' doon;

'Summat to drink—sa' 'ot?' I 'a nowt but Adam's
  wine:

What's the 'eät o' this little 'ill-side to the 'eät o' the line?

---

[1] The vowels *aï*, pronounced separately though in the
closest conjunction, best render the sound of the long *i* and *y*
in this dialect.   But since such words as *craïin'*, *daïin'*, *whaï*,
aï(I), &c., look awkward except in a page of express phonetics,
I have thought it better to leave the simple *i* and *y*, and to
trust that my readers will give them the broader pronuncia-
tion.
[2] The *oo* short, as in 'wood.'

II.

'What's i' tha bottle a-stanning theer?'   I'll tell tha.

    Gin.

But if thou wants thy grog, tha mun goä fur it down

    to the inn.

Naay—fur I be maäin-glad, but thaw tha was iver sa

    dry,

Thou gits naw gin fro' the bottle theer, an' I'll tell

    tha wny.

III.

Meü an' thy sister was married, when wur it? back-

    end o' June,

Ten year sin', and wa 'greed as well as a fiddle i' tune:

I could fettle and clump owd booöts and shoes wi' the

    best on 'em all,

As fer as fro' Thursby thurn hup to Harmsby and

    Hutterby Hall.

We was busy as beeäs i' the bloom an' as 'appy as
'art could think,

An' then the babby wur burn, and then I taäkes to
the drink.

IV.

An' I weünt gaäinsaäy it, my lad, thaw I be hafe
shaämed on it now,

We could sing a good song at the Plow, we could
sing a good song at the Plow ;

Thaw once of a frosty night I slither'd an' hurted my
huck,[1]

An' I coom'd neck-an-crop soomtimes slaäpe down i'
the squad an' the muck :

An' once I fowt wi' the Taäilor—not hafe ov a man,
my lad—

Fur he scrawm'd an' scratted my faäce like a cat, an'
it maäde 'er sa mad

---

[1] Hip.

That Sally she turn'd a tongue-banger,[1] an' raäted ma,

  'Sottin' thy braäins

Guzzlin' an' soäkin' an' smoäkin' an' hawmin'[2] about

  i' the laanes, -

Soä sow-droonk that thá doesn not touch thy 'at to

  the Squire;'

An' I looök'd cock-eyed at my noäse an' I seeäd 'im a-

  gittin' o' fire;

But sin' I wur hallus i' liquor an' hallus as droonk as

  a king,

Foälks' coostom flitted awaäy like a kite wi' a brokken

  string.

V.

An' Sally she wesh'd foälks' cloäths to keep the wolf

  fro' the door,

Eh but the moor she riled me, she druv me to drink

  the moor,

---

[1] Scold.　　　　　　　[2] Lounging.

Fur I fun', when 'er back wur turn'd, wheer Sally's
    owd stockin' wur 'id,
An' I grabb'd the munny she maäde, and I weär'd_it
    o' liquor, I did.

VI.

An' one night I cooms 'oäm like a bull gotten_loose at
    a fuäir,
An' she wur a-waäitin' fo'mma, an' cryin' and teärin'
    'er 'aäir,
An' I tummled athurt the craädle an' sweär'd as I'd
    breäk ivry stick
O' furnitur 'ere i' the 'ouse, an' I gied our Sally a kick,
An' I mash'd the taübles an' chairs, an' she an' the
    babby beäl'd,[1]
Fur I knaw'd naw moor what I did nor a mortal
    beäst o' the feäld.

---

[1] Bellowed, cried out.

VII.

An' when I waäked i' the murnin' I seeäd that our
Sally went laämed

Cos' o' the kick as I gied er, an' I wur dreädful
ashaämed ;

An' Sally wur sloomy [1] an' draggle-taäil'd in an owd
turn gown,

An' the babby's faäce wurn't wesh'd an' the 'ole 'ouse
hupside down.

VIII.

An' then I minded our Sally sa pratty an' neät an
sweeät,

Straït as a pole an' cleän as a flower fro' 'eäd to feeät :

An' then I minded the fust kiss I gied 'er by Thursby
thurn ;

Theer wur a lark a-singin' 'is best of a Sunday at
murn,

---

[1] Sluggish, out of spirits.

Couldn't see 'im, we 'eärd im a-mountin' oop 'igher
an' 'igher,

An' then 'e turn'd to the sun, an' 'e shined like a
sparkle o' fire.

'Doesn't tha see 'im,' she axes, 'fur I can see 'im?'
an I

Seeäd nobbut the smile o' the sun as danced in 'er
pratty blue eye;

An' I says 'I mun gie tha a kiss,' an' Sally says
'Noä, thou moänt,'

But I gied 'er a kiss, an' then anoother, an' Sally says
'doänt!'

IX.

An' when we coom'd into Meeätin', at fust she wur
all in a tew,

But, arter, we sing'd the 'ymn togither like birds on a
beugh;

An' Muggins 'e preäch'd o' Hell-fire an' the loov o'

God fur men,

An' then upo' coomin' awaäy Sally gied me a kiss ov

'ersen.

X.

Heer wur a fall fro' a kiss to a kick like Saätan as fell

Down out o' heaven i' Hell-fire—thaw theer's naw

drinkin' i' Hell ;

Meä fur to kick our Sally as kep the wolf fro' the

door,

All along o' the drink, fur I loov'd 'er as well as afoor.

XI.

Sa like a graät num-cumpus I blubber'd awaäy o' the

bed—

'Weänt niver do it naw moor ; ' an' Sally looökt up an'

she said,

'I'll upowd it [1] tha weünt; thou'rt laike the rest o' the
    men,

Thou'll goä sniffin' about the tap till tha does it agëan.

Theer's thy hennemy, man, an' I knaws, as knaws tha
    sa well,

That, if tha seeäs 'im an' smells 'im tha'll foller 'im
    slick into Hell.'

XII.

'Naäy,' says I, 'fur I weünt goä sniffin' about the
    tap.'

'Weünt tha?' she says, an' mysen I thowt i' mysen
    'mayhap.'

'Noa:' an' I started awaäy like a shot, an' down to
    the Hinn,

An' I browt what tha seeäs stannin' theer, yon big
    black bottle o' gin.

---

[1] I'll uphold it.

XIII.

'That caps owt,' [1] says Sally, an' saw she begins to cry,

But I puts it inter 'er 'ands an' I says to 'er, ' Sally,'
    says I,

' Stan' 'im theer i' the naäme o' the Lord an' the
    power ov 'is Graäce,   .

Stan' 'im theer, fur I'll looök my hennemy straït i' the
    faäce,

Stan' 'im theer i' the winder, an' let ma looök at 'im
    then,

E' seeäms naw moor nor watter, an' 'e's the Divil's
    oän sen.'

XIV.

An' I wur down i' tha mouth, couldn't do naw work
    an' all,

Nasty an' snaggy an' shaäky, an' poonch'd my 'and wi'
    the hawl,

---

[1] That's beyond everything.

But she wur a power o' coomfut, an' sattled 'ersen o'
　　my knee,

An' coäxd an' coodled me oop till agëan I feel'd mysen
　　free.

XV.

An' Sally she tell'd it about, an' foälk stood a-gawmin' [1]
　　in,

As thaw it wur summat bewitch'd istead of a quart o'
　　gin;

An' some on 'em said it wur watter—an' I wur
　　chousin' the wife,

Fur I couldn't 'owd 'ands off gin, wur it nobbut to
　　saave my life;

An' blacksmith 'e strips me the thick ov 'is airm, an'
　　'e shaws it to me,

' Feëal thou this! thou can't graw this upo' watter!'
　　says he.

_____

[1] Staring vacantly.

An' Doctor 'e calls o' Sunday an' just as candles was
    lit,

'Thou moänt do it,' he says, 'tha mun breäk 'im off
    bit by bit.'

'Thou'rt but a Methody-man,' says Parson, and laäys
    down 'is 'at,

An' 'e points to the bottle o' gin, 'but I respecks tha
    fur that;'

An' Squire, his oän very sen, walks down fro' the 'All
    to see,

An' 'e spanks 'is 'and into mine, 'fur I respecks tha,'
    says 'e;

An' coostom ageän draw'd in like a wind fro' far an'
    wide,

And browt me the booöts to be cobbled fro' hafe the
    coontryside.

XVI

An' theer 'e stans an' theer 'e shall stan to my dying
daäy;

I 'a gotten to loov 'im ageän in anoother kind of a
waäy,

Proud on 'im, like, my lad, an' I keeäps 'im cleän an'
bright,

Loovs 'im, an' roobs 'im, an' doosts 'im, an' puts 'im
back i' the light.

XVII.

Wouldn't a pint a' sarved as well as a quart   Naw
doubt :

But I liked a bigger feller to fight wi' an' fowt it out.

Fine an' meller 'e mun be by this, if I cared to taäste,

But I moänt, my lad, and I weänt, fur I'd feäl mysen
cleän disgraäced.

XVIII.

An' once I said to the Missis, ' My lass, when I cooms
to die,

Smash the bottle to smithers, the Divil's in 'im,'
said I.

But arter I chaänged my mind, an' if Sally be left
aloän,

I'll hev 'im a-buried wi'mma an' taäke 'im afoor the
Throän.

XIX.

Coom thou 'eer—yon laädy a-steppin' along the
streeät,

Doesn't tha knaw 'er—sa pratty, an' feät, an' neät,
an' sweeät?

Look at the cloäths on 'er back, thebbe ammost
spick-span-new,

An' Tommy's faäce is as fresh as a codlin 'at's wesh'd
i' the dew.

XX.

'Ere's our Sally an' Tommy, an' we be a-goin to dine,

Baäcon an' taätes, an' a beslings-puddin' [1] an' Adam's

   wine;

But if tha wants ony grog tha mun goä fur it down

   to the Hinn,

Fur I weänt shed a drop on 'is blood, noa, not fur

   Sally's oän kin.

---

[1] A pudding made with the first milk of the cow after calving.

THE REVENGE.

A Ballad of the Fleet.

I.

At Flores in the Azores Sir Richard Grenville lay,

And a pinnace, like a flutter'd bird, came flying from

far away :

'Spanish ships of war at sea ! we have sighted fifty-

three !'

Then sware Lord Thomas Howard : ''Fore God I am

no coward ;

But I cannot meet them here, for my ships are out of

gear,

And the half my men are sick. I must fly, but follow

quick.

We are six ships of the line; can we fight with fifty-

three ?'

II.

Then spake Sir Richard Grenville : ' I know you are

no coward ;

You fly them for a moment to fight with them again.

But I've ninety men and more that are lying sick

ashore.

I should count myself the coward if I left them, my

Lord Howard,

To these Inquisition dogs and the devildoms of Spain.'

III.

So Lord Howard past away with five ships of war

that day,

Till he melted like a cloud in the silent. summer

heaven;

But Sir Richard bore in hand all his sick men from
      the land

Very carefully and slow,

Men of Bideford in Devon,

And we laid them on the ballast down below;

For we brought them all aboard,

And they blest him in their pain, that they were not
      left to Spain,'

To the thumbscrew and the stake, for the glory of the
      Lord.

IV.

He had only a hundred seamen to work the ship and
      to fight,

And he sailed away from Flores till the Spaniard
      came in sight,

With his huge sea-castles heaving upon the weather
      bow.

' Shall we fight or shall we fly ?

Good Sir Richard, tell us now,

For to fight is but to die !

There'll be little of us left by the time this sun be set.'

And Sir Richard said again : ' We be all good
English men.

Let us bang these dogs of Seville, the children of the
devil,

For I never turn'd my back upon Don or devil yet.'

v.

Sir Richard spoke and he laugh'd, and we roar'd a
hurrah, and so

The little Revenge ran on sheer into the heart of
the foe,

With her hundred fighters on deck, and her ninety
sick below ;

For half of their fleet to the right and half to the left
were seen,

And the little Revenge ran on thro' the long sea-
lane between.

VI.

Thousands of their soldiers look'd down from their
decks and laugh'd,

Thousands of their seamen made mock at the mad
little craft

Running on and on, till delay'd

By their mountain-like San Philip that, of fifteen
hundred tons,

And up-shadowing high above us with her yawning
tiers of guns,

Took the breath from our sails, and we stay'd.

VII.

And while now the great San Philip hung above us

    like a cloud

Whence the thunderbolt will fall

Long and loud,

Four galleons drew away

From the Spanish fleet that day,

And two upon the larboard and two upon the star-

    board lay,

And the battle-thunder broke from them all.

VIII.

But anon the great San Philip, she bethought her-

    self and went

Having that within her womb that had left her ill

    content ;

And the rest they came aboard us, and they fought

    us hand to hand,

For a dozen times they came with their pikes and
musqueteers,

And a dozen times we shook 'em off as a dog that
shakes his ears

When he leaps from the water to the land.

IX.

And the sun went down, and the stars came out far
over the summer sea,

But never a moment ceased the fight of the one and
the fifty-three.

Ship after ship, the whole night long, their high-built
galleons came,

Ship after ship, the whole night long, with her battle-
thunder and flame;

Ship after ship, the whole night long, drew back with
her dead and her shame.

For some were sunk and many were shatter'd, and so

    could fight us no more—

God of battles, was ever a battle like this in the world

    before?

X.

For he said ' Fight on ! fight on ! '

Tho' his vessel was all but a wreck ;

And it chanced that, when half of the short summer

    night was gone,

With a grisly wound to be drest he had left the deck,

But a bullet struck him that was dressing it suddenly

    dead,

And himself he was wounded again in the side and

    the head,

And he said ' Fight on ! fight on ! '

XI.

And the night went down, and the sun smiled out far
over the summer sea,

And the Spanish fleet with broken sides lay round us
all in a ring;

But they dared not touch us again, for they fear'
that we still could sting,

So they watch'd what the end would be.

And we had not fought them in vain,

But in perilous plight were we,

Seeing forty of our poor hundred were slain,

And half of the rest of us maim'd for life

In the crash of the cannonades and the desperate
strife;

And the sick men down in the hold were most of
them stark and cold,

And the pikes were all broken or bent, and the powder
was all of it spent;

And the masts and the rigging were lying over the
side;

But Sir Richard cried in his English pride,

‘ We have fought such a fight for a day and a night

As may never be fought again !

We have won great glory, my men ! .

And a day less or more

At sea or ashore,

We die—does it matter when ?

Sink me the ship, Master Gunner—sink her, split her
in twain !

Fall into the hands of God, not into the hands of
Spain !’

XII.

And the gunner said ‘ Ay, ay,’ but the seamen made
reply :

‘ We have children, we have wives,

And the Lord hath spared our lives.

E

We will make the Spaniard promise, if we yield, to

let us go ;

We shall live to fight again and to strike another

blow.'

And the lion there lay dying, and they yielded to the

foe.

XIII.

And the stately Spanish men to their flagship bore

him then,

Where they laid him by the mast, old Sir Richard

caught at last,

And they praised him to his face with their courtly

foreign grace ;

But he rose upon their decks, and he cried :

'I have fought for Queen and Faith like a valiant

man and true ;

I have only done my duty as a man is bound to do :

With a joyful spirit I Sir Richard Grenville die ! '

And he fell upon their decks, and he died.

XIV.

And they stared at the dead that had been so valiant

and true,

And had holden the power and glory of Spain so.

cheap

That he dared her with one little ship and his English.

few ;

Was he devil or man ?   He was devil for aught they

knew,

But they sank his body with honour down into the

deep,

And they mann'd the Revenge with a swarthier

alien crew,

And away she sail'd with her loss and long'd for her

own ;

When a wind from the lands they had ruin'd awoke
from sleep,

And the water began to heave and the weather to
moan,

And or ever that evening ended a great gale blew,

And a wave like the wave that is raised by an earthquake grew,

Till it smote on their hulls and their sails and their
masts and their flags,

And the whole sea plunged and fell on the shot-
shatter'd navy of Spain,

And the little Revenge herself went down by the
island crags

To be lost evermore in the main.

THE SISTERS.

THEY have left the doors ajar; and by their clash,

And prelude on the keys, I know the song,

Their favourite—which I call ' The Tables Turned.'

Evelyn begins it ' O diviner Air.'

EVELYN.

O diviner Air,

Thro' the heat, the drowth, the dust, the glare,

Far from out the west in shadowing showers,

Over all the meadow baked and bare,

Making fresh and fair

All the bowers and the flowers,

Fainting flowers, faded bowers,

Over all this weary world of ours,

Breathe, diviner Air !

A sweet voice that—you scarce could better that.

Now follows Edith echoing Evelyn.

EDITH.

O diviner light,

Thro' the cloud that roofs our noon with night,

Thro' the blotting mist, the blinding showers,

Far from out a sky for ever bright,

Over all the woodland's flooded bowers,

Over all the meadow's drowning flowers,

Over all this ruin'd world of ours,

Break diviner light !

Marvellously like, their voices—and themselves !

Tho' one is somewhat deeper than the other,

As one is somewhat graver than the other—

Edith than Evelyn. Your good Uncle, whom

You count the father of your fortune, longs

For this alliance : let me ask you then,

Which voice most takes you ? for I do not doubt

Being a watchful parent, you are taken

With one or other : tho' sometimes I fear

You may be flickering, fluttering in a doubt

Between the two—which must not be—which might

Be death to one : they both are beautiful :

Evelyn is gayer, wittier, prettier, says

The common voice, if one may trust it : she ?

No ! but the paler and the graver, Edith.

Woo her and gain her then : no wavering, boy !

The graver is perhaps the one for you

Who jest and laugh so easily and so well.

For love will go by contrast, as by likes.

No sisters ever prized each other more.
Not so : their mother and her sister loved
More passionately still.

        But that my best
And oldest friend, your Uncle, wishes it,
And that I know you worthy everyway
To be my son, I might, perchance, be loath
To part them, or part from them : and yet one
Should marry, or all the broad lands in your view
From this bay window—which our house has held
Three hundred years—will pass collaterally.

        My father with a child on either knee,
A hand upon the head of either child,
Smoothing their locks, as golden as his own
Were silver, 'get them wedded' would he say.
And once my prattling Edith ask'd him ' why ? '
Ay, why ? said he, ' for why should I go lame ? '

Then told them of his wars, and of his wound.

For see—this wine—the grape from whence it flow'd

Was blackening on the slopes of Portugal,

When that brave soldier, down the terrible ridge

Plunged in the last fierce charge at Waterloo,

And caught the laming bullet. He left me this,

Which yet retains a memory of its youth,

As I of mine, and my first passion. Come !

Here's to your happy union with my child !

Yet must you change your name : no fault of mine !

You say that you can do it as willingly

As birds make ready for their bridal-time

By change of feather : for all that, my boy,

Some birds are sick and sullen when they moult.

An old and worthy name ! but mine that stirr'd

Among our civil wars and earlier too

Among the Roses, the more venerable.

I care not for a name—no fault of mine.

Once more—a happier marriage than my own !

　　You see yon Lombard poplar on the plain.

The highway running by it leaves a breadth

Of sward to left and right, where, long ago,

One bright May morning in a world of song,

I lay at leisure, watching overhead

The aërial poplar wave, an amber spire.

　　I dozed ; I woke.　An open landaulet

Whirl'd by, which, after it had past me, show'd

Turning my way, the loveliest face on earth.

The face of one there sitting opposite,

On whom I brought a strange unhappiness,

That time I did not see.

　　　　　　　　　　　Love at first sight

May seem—with goodly rhyme and reason for it—

Possible—at first glimpse, and for a face

Gone in a moment—strange.   Yet once, when first

I came on lake Llanberris in the dark,

A moonless night with storm—one lightning-fork

Flash'd out the lake ; and tho' I loiter'd there

The full day after, yet in retrospect

That less than momentary thunder-sketch

Of lake and mountain conquers all the day.

   The Sun himself has limn'd the face for me.

Not quite so quickly, no, nor half as well.

For look you here—the shadows are too deep,

And like the critic's blurring comment make

The veriest beauties of the work appear

The darkest faults : the sweet eyes frown : the

      lips

Seem but a gash.   My sole memorial

Of Edith—no the other,—both indeed.

So that bright face was flash'd thro' sense and

    soul

And by the poplar vanish'd—to be found

Long after, as it seem'd, beneath the tall

Tree-bowers, and those long-sweeping beechen boughs

Of our New Forest.   I was there alone :

The phantom of the whirling landaulet

For ever past me by : when one quick peal

Of laughter drew me thro' the glimmering glades

Down to the snowlike sparkle of a cloth

On fern and foxglove.   Lo, the face again,

My Rosalind in this Arden—Edith—all

One bloom of youth, health, beauty, happiness,

And moved to merriment at a passing jest.

There one of those about her knowing me

Call'd me to join them ; so with these I spent

What seem'd my crowning hour, my day of days.

I woo'd her then, nor unsuccessfully,

The worse for her, for me! was I content ?

Ay—no, not quite; for now and then I thought

Laziness, vague love-longings, the bright May,

Had made a heated haze to magnify

The charm of Edith—that a man's ideal

Is high in Heaven, and lodged with Plato's God,'

Not findable here—content, and not content,

In some such fashion as a man may be

That having had the portrait of his friend

Drawn by an artist, looks at it, and says,

' Good! very like! not altogether he.'

As yet I had not bound myself by words,

Only, believing I loved Edith, made

Edith love *me*.   Then came the day when I,

Flattering myself that all my doubts were fools

Born of the fool this Age that doubts of all—

Not I that day of Edith's love or mine—

Had braced my purpose to declare myself:

I stood upon the stairs of Paradise.

The golden gates would open at a word.

I spoke it—told her of my passion, seen

And lost and found again, had got so far,

Had caught her hand, her eyelids fell—I heard

Wheels, and a noise of welcome at the doors—

On a sudden after two Italian years

Had set the blossom of her health again,

The younger sister, Evelyn, enter'd—there,

There was the face, and altogether she.

The mother fell about the daughter's neck,

The sisters closed in one another's arms,

Their people throng'd about them from the hall,

And in the thick of question and reply

I fled the house, driven by one angel face,

And all the Furies.

I was bound to her ;

I could not free myself in honour—bound

Not by the sounded letter of the word,

But counterpressures of the yielded hand

That timorously and faintly echoed mine,

Quick blushes, the sweet dwelling of her eyes

Upon me when she thought I did not see—

Were these not bonds ? nay, nay, but could I wed her

Loving the other ? do her that great wrong ?

Had I not dream'd I loved her yestermorn ?

Had I not known where Love, at first a fear,

Grew after marriage to full height and form ?

Yet after marriage, that mock-sister there—

Brother-in-law—the fiery nearness of it—

Unlawful and disloyal brotherhood—

What end but darkness could ensue from this

For all the three ?   So Love and Honour jarr'd

Tho' Love and Honour join'd to raise the full

High-tide of doubt that sway'd me up and down

Advancing nor retreating.

                              Edith wrote :

' My mother bids me ask' (I did not tell you—

A widow with less guile than many a child.

God help the wrinkled children that are Christ's

As well as the plump cheek—she wrought us harm,

Poor soul, not knowing) 'are you ill? (so ran

The letter) 'you have not been here of late.

You will not find me here.   At last I go

On that long-promised visit to the North.

I told your wayside story to my mother

And Evelyn.   She remembers you.   Farewell.

Pray come and see my mother.   Almost blind

With ever-growing cataract, yet she thinks

She sees you when she hears.   Again farewell.'

Cold words from one I had hoped to warm so far

That I could stamp my image on her heart !

'Pray come and see my mother, and farewell.'

Cold, but as welcome as free airs of heaven

After a dungeon's closeness.   Selfish, strange !

What dwarfs are men ! my strangled vanity

Utter'd a stifled cry—to have vext myself

And all in vain for her—cold heart or none—

No bride for me.   Yet so my path was clear

To win the sister.

                Whom I woo'd and won.

For Evelyn knew not of my former suit,

Because the simple mother work'd upon

By Edith pray'd me not to whisper of it.

And Edith would be bridesmaid on the day.

But on that day, not being all at ease,

I from the altar glancing back upon her,

Before the first ' I will ' was utter'd, saw

The bridesmaid pale, statuelike, passionless—

F

'No harm, no harm' I turn'd again, and placed

My ring upon the finger of my bride.

So, when we parted, Edith spoke no word,

She wept no tear, but round my Evelyn clung

In utter silence for so long, I thought

'What will she never set her sister free?'

We left her, happy each in each, and then,

As tho' the happiness of each in each

Were not enough, must fain have torrents, lakes.

Hills, the great things of Nature and the fair,

To lift us as it were from commonplace,

And help us to our joy. Better have sent

Our Edith thro' the glories of the earth,

To change with her horizon, if true Love

Were not his own imperial all-in-all.

Far off we went. My God, I would not live

Save that I think this gross hard-seeming world

Is our misshaping vision of the Powers

Behind the world, that make our griefs our gains.

For on the dark night of our marriage-day

The great Tragedian, that had quench'd herself

In that assumption of the bridesmaid—she

That loved me—our true Edith—her brain broke

With over-acting, till she rose and fled

Beneath a pitiless rush of Autumn rain

To the deaf church—to be let in—to pray

Before *that* altar—so I think; and there

They found her beating the hard Protestant doors.

She died and she was buried ere we knew.

I learnt it first. I had to speak. At once

The bright quick smile of Evelyn, that had sunn'd

The morning of our marriage, past away :

And on our home-return the daily want

Of Edith in the house, the garden, still

Haunted us like her ghost ; and by and by,

Either from that necessity for talk

Which lives with blindness, or plain innocence

Of nature, or desire that her lost child

Should earn from both the praise of heroism,

The mother broke her promise to the dead,

And told the living daughter with what love

Edith had welcomed my brief wooing of her,

And all her sweet self-sacrifice and death.

　　Henceforth that mystic bond betwixt the twins—

Did I not tell you they were twins?—prevail'd

So far that no caress could win my wife

Back to that passionate answer of full heart

I had from her at first.　Not that her love,

Tho' scarce as great as Edith's power of love,

Had lessen'd, but the mother's garrulous wail

For ever woke the unhappy Past again,

Till that dead bridesmaid, meant to be my bride,

Put forth cold hands between us, and I fear'd

The very fountains of her life were chill'd ;

So took her thence, and brought her here, and here

She bore a child, whom reverently we call'd

Edith ; and in the second year was born

A second—this I named from her own self,

Evelyn ; then two weeks—no more—she joined,

In and beyond the grave, that one she loved.

Now in this quiet of declining life,

Thro' dreams by night and trances of the day,

The sisters glide about me hand in hand,

Both beautiful alike, nor can I tell

One from the other, no, nor care to tell

One from the other, only know they come,

They smile upon me, till, remembering all

The love they both have borne me, and the love

I bore them both—divided as I am

From either by the stillness of the grave—

I know not which of these I love the best.

But *you* love Edith; and her own true eyes

Are traitors to her; our quick Evelyn—

The merrier, prettier, wittier, as they talk,

And not without good reason, my good son—

Is yet untouch'd : and I that hold them both

Dearest of all things—well, I am not sure—

But if there lie a preference eitherway,

And in the rich.vocabulary of Love

' Most dearest ' be a true superlative—

I think *I* likewise love your Edith most.

THE VILLAGE WIFE; OR, THE ENTAIL.[1]

I.

'Ouse-keeper sent tha my lass, fur New Squire coom'd
last night.

Butter an' heggs—yis—yis. I'll goä wi' tha back : all
right;

Butter I warrants be prime, an' I warrants the heggs
be as well,

Hafe a pint o' milk runs out when ya breäks the shell.

II.

Sit thysen down fur a bit : hev a glass o' cowslip wine !

I liked the owd Squire an' 'is gells as thaw they was
gells o' mine,

---

[1] See note to 'Northern Cobbler.'

Fur then we was all es one, the Squire an' 'is darters an' me,

Hall but Miss Annie, the heldest, I niver not took t she :

But Nelly, the last of the cletch,[1] I liked 'er the fust on 'em all,

Fur hoffens we talkt o' my darter es died o' the fever at fall :

An' I thowt 'twur the will o' the Lord, but Miss Annie she said it wur draäins,

Fur she hedn't naw coomfut in 'er, an' arn'd naw thanks fur 'er paäins.

Eh ! thebbe all wi' the Lord my childer, I han't gotten none !

Sa new Squire's coom'd wi' 'is taäil in 'is 'and, an' owd Squire's gone.

---

[1] A brood of chickens.

III.

Fur 'staäte be i' taäil, my lass: tha dosn' knaw what

that be ?

But I knaws the law, I does, for the lawyer ha towd

it me.

' When theer's naw 'eäd to a 'Ouse by the fault o' that

ere maäle—

The gells they counts fur nowt, and the next un he

taäkes the taäil.'

IV.

What be the next un like ? can tha tell ony harm on

'im lass ?—

Naay sit down—naw 'urry—sa cowd !—hev another

glass !

Straänge an' cowd fur the time ! we may happen a

fall o' snaw—

Not es I cares fur to hear ony harm, but I likes to

knaw.

An' I 'oäps es 'e beänt boooklarn'd : but 'e dosn not
coom fro' the shere ;

We'd anew o' that wi' the Squire, an' we haätes boook-
larnin' ere.

V.

Fur Squire wur a Varsity scholard, an' niver lookt
arter the land—

Whoäts or turmuts or taätes—'e 'ed hallus a booök i'
'is 'and,

Hallus aloän wi' 'is boooks, thaw nigh upo' seventy
year.

An' boooks, what's boooks ? thou knaws thebbe neyther 'ere nor theer.

VI.

An' the gells, they hedn't naw taäils, an' the lawyer he
towd it me

That 'is taiil were soä tied up es he couldn't cut down
a tree !

'Drat the trees,' says I, to be sewer I haätes 'em, my
    lass,

Fur we puts the muck o' the land, an' they sucks the
    muck fro' the grass.

VII.

An' Squire wur hallus a-smilin', an' gied to the tramps
    goin' by—

An' all o' the wust i' the parish—wi' hoffens a drop in
    'is eye.

An' ivry darter o' Squire's hed her awn ridin-erse to
    'ersen,

An' they rampaged about wi' their grooms, an' was
    'untin' arter the men,

An' hallus a-dallackt [1] an' dizen'd out, an' a-buyin' new
    cloäthes,

While 'e sit like a graät glimmer-gowk [2] wi' 'is glasses
    athurt 'is noäse,

---

[1] Overdrest in gay colours.   [2] Owl.

An' 'is noäse sa grufted wi' snuff es it couldn't be
scroob'd awaäy,

Fur atween 'is reädin' an' writin' 'e snifft up a box in
a daäy,

An' 'e niver runn'd arter the fox, nor arter the birds
wi' 'is gun,

An' 'e niver not shot one 'are, but 'e leäved it to
Charlie 'is son,

An' 'e niver not fish'd 'is awn ponds, but Charlie 'e
cotch'd the pike,

Fur 'e warn't not burn to the land, an' 'e didn't take
kind to it like;

But I eärs es 'e'd gie fur a howry [1] owd book thutty
pound an' moor,

An' 'e'd wrote an owd book, his awn sen, sa I knaw'd
es 'e'd coom to be poor;

---

[1] Filthy.

An' 'e gied—I be fear'd fur to tell tha 'ow much—fur
an owd scratted stoän,

An' 'e digg'd up a loomp i' the land an' 'e got a brown
pot an' a boän,

An' 'e bowt owd money, es wouldn't goä, wi' good
gowd o' the Queen,

An' 'e bowt little statutes all-naäkt an' which was a
shaame to be seen ;

But 'e niver looükt ower a bill, nor 'e niver not seed
to owt,

An' 'e niver knawd nowt but boooks, an' boooks, as
thou knaws, beänt nowt.

VIII.

But owd Squire's laädy es long es she lived she kep
'em all clear,

Thaw es long es she lived I niver hed none of 'er
darters 'ere ;

But arter she died we was all es one, the childer
an' me,

An' sarvints runn'd in an' out, an' offens we hed 'em
to tea.

Lawk! 'ow I laugh'd when the lasses 'ud talk o' their
Missis's waäys,

An' the Missisis talk'd o' the lasses.—I'll tell tha
some o' these daäys.

Hoänly Miss Annie were saw stuck oop, like 'er
mother afoor—

'Er an' 'er blessed daiter—they niver derken'd my
door.

IX.

An' Squire 'e smiled an' e' smiled till 'e 'd gotten a
fright at last,

An' 'e calls fur 'is son, fur the 'turney's letters they
foller'd sa fast;

But Squire wur afear'd o' 'is son, an' 'e says to 'im,

    meek as a mouse,

'Lad, thou mun cut off thy taäil, or the gells 'ull goä

    to the 'Ouse,

Fur I finds es I be that i' debt, es I 'oäps es thou'll

    'elp me a bit,

An' if thou'll 'gree to cut off thy taäil I may saäve

    mysen yit.'

X.

But Charlie 'e sets back 'is ears, an' 'e sweärs, an' 'e

    says to 'im ' Noa.'

' I've gotten the 'staäte by the taäil an' be dang'd if I

    iver let goa !

Coom ! coom ! feyther,' 'e says, 'why shouldn't thy

    booöks be sowd ?

I hears es soom o' thy booöks mebbe worth their weight

    i' gowd.'

XI.

Heäps 'an' heäps o' booöks, I ha' see'd 'em, belong'd
  to the Squire,

But the lasses 'ed teärd out leaves i' the middle to
  kindle the fire ;

Sa moäst on 'is owd big booöks fetch'd nigh to nowt
  at the saäle,

And Squire were at Charlie ageän to git 'im to cut
  off 'is taäi!.

XII.

Ya wouldn't find Charlie's likes—'e were that out-
  dacious at 'oäm,

Not thaw ya went fur to raäke out Hell wi' a small-
  tooth coämb—

Droonk wi' the Quoloty's wine, an' droonk wi' the
  farmer's aäle,

Mad wi' the lasses an' all—an' 'e wouldn't cut off the
  taäil.

XIII.

Thou's coom'd oop by the beck ; and a thurn be
a-grawin' theer,

I niver ha seed it sa white wi' the Maüy es I see'd it
to-year—

Theerabouts Charlie joompt—and it gied me a scare
tother night,

Fur I thowt it wur Charlie's ghoäst i' the derk, fur
it looökt sa white.

' Billy,' says 'e, ' hev a joomp !'—thaw the banks o
the beck be sa high,

Fur he ca'd 'is 'erse Billy-rough-un, thaw niver a hair
wur awry ;

But Billy fell bakkuds o' Charlie, an' Charlie 'e brok
'is neck,

So theer wur a hend o' the taäil, fur 'e lost 'is taäil i'
the beck.

G

XIV.

Sa 'is taäil wur lost an' 'is booöks wur gone an' 'is boy

wur deäd,

An' Squire 'e smiled an' 'e smiled, but 'e niver not

lift oop 'is eäd :

Hallus a soft un Squire! an' 'e smiled, fur 'e hedn't

naw friend,

Sa feyther an' son was buried togither, an' this wur

the hend.

XV.

An' Parson as hesn't the call, nor the mooney, but

hes the pride,

'E reäds of a sewer an' sartan 'oäp o' the tother side ;

But I beänt that sewer es the Lord, howsiver they

praäy'd an' praäy'd,

Lets them inter 'eaven eäsy es leäves their debts to

be paäid.

Siver the mou'ds rattled down upo' poor owd Squire
  i' the wood,

An' I cried along wi' the gells, fur they weänt niver
  coom to naw good.

XVI.

Fur Molly the youngest she walkt awaäy wi' a hoffi-
  cer lad,

An' nawbody 'eärd on 'er sin, sa o' coorse she be gone
  to the bad !

An' Lucy wur laäme o' one leg, sweet-'arts she niver
  'ed none—

Straänge an' unheppen [1] Miss Lucy ! we naämed her
  ' Dot an' gaw one ! '

An' Hetty wur weak i' the hattics, wi'out ony harm
  i' the legs,

An' the fever 'ed baäked Jinny's 'eäd as bald as one o'
  them heggs,

---

[1] Ungainly, awkward.

An' Nelly wur up fro' the craädle as big i' the mouth

as a cow,

'An' saw she mun hammergrate,¹ lass, or she weünt git

a maäte onyhow !

An' es fur Miss Annie es call'd me afoor my awn

foälks to my faäce

' A hignorant village wife as 'ud hev to be larn'd her

awn plaäce,'

Hes fur Miss Hannie the heldest hes now be a-grawin'

sa howd,

I knaws that mooch o' sheä, es it beänt not fit to be

towd !

XVII.

Sa I didn't not taäke it kindly ov owd Miss Annie to

saäy

Es I should be talkin ageän 'em, es soon es they went

awaäy,

¹ Emigrate.

Fur, lawks! 'ow I cried when they went, an' our
    Nelly she gied me 'er 'and,

Fur I'd ha done owt fur the Squire an' 'is gells es
    belong'd to the land;

Boooks, es I said afoor, thebbe neyther 'ere nor theer!

But I sarved 'em wi' butter an' heggs fur huppuds o'
    twenty year.

XVIII.

An' they hallus paäid what I hax'd, sa I hallus deal'd
    wi' the Hall,

An' they knaw'd what butter wur, an' they knaw'd
    what a hegg wur an' all;

Hugger-mugger they lived, but they wasn't that eäsy
    to pleäse,

Till I gied 'em Hinjian curn, an' they laäid big heggs
    es tha seeas;

An' I niver puts saäme [1] i' *my* butter, they does it at
Willis's farm,

Taäste another drop o' the wine—tweänt do tha naw
harm.

XIX.

Sa new Squire's coom'd wi' 'is taäil in 'is 'and, an'
owd Squire's gone;

I heard 'im a roomlin' by, but arter my nightcap wur
on;

Sa I han't clapt eyes on 'im yit, fur he coom'd last
night sa laäte—

Pluksh!!![2] the hens i' the peïs! why didn't tha hesp
the gaäte?

---

[1] Lard.

[2] A cry accompanied by a clapping of hands to scare
trespassing fowl.

IN THE CHILDREN'S HOSPITAL.

EMMIE.

I.

OUR doctor had call'd in another, I never had seen
    him before,

But he sent a chill to my heart when I saw him come
    in at the door,

Fresh from the surgery-schools of France and of other
    lands—

Harsh red hair, big voice, big chest, big merciless
    hands !

Wonderful cures he had done, O yes, but they said too
    of him

He was happier using the knife than in trying to save

    the limb,

And that I can well believe, for he look'd so coarse

    and so red,

I could think he was one of those who would break

    their jests on the dead,

And mangle the living dog that had loved him and

    fawn'd at his knee—

Drench'd with the hellish oorali—that ever such

    things should be !

II.

Here was a boy—I am sure that some of our children

    would die

But for the voice of Love, and the smile, and the

    comforting eye—

Here was a boy in the ward, every bone seem'd out of

    its place—

Caught in a mill and crush'd—it was all but a hopeless case :

And he handled him gently enough; but his voice
and his face were not kind,

And it was but a hopeless case, he had seen it and
made up his mind,

And he said to me roughly 'The lad will need little
more of your care.'

'All the more need,' I told him, 'to seek the Lord
Jesus in prayer ;

They are all his children here, and I pray for them all
as my own :'

But he turn'd to me, ' Ay, good woman, can prayer
set a broken bone ? '

Then he mutter'd half to himself, but I know that I
heard him say

' All very well—but the good Lord Jesus has had his
day.'

III.

Had? has it come? It has only dawn'd. It will come
by and by.

O how could I serve in the wards if the hope of the
world were a lie?

How could I bear with the sights and the loathsome
smells of disease

But that He said Ye do it to me, when ye do it to
these'?

IV.

So he went. And we past to this ward where the
younger children are laid :

Here is the cot of our orphan, our darling, our meek
little maid;

Empty you see just now ! We have lost her who loved
her so much—

Patient of pain tho' as quick as a sensitive plant to
the touch ;

Hers was the prettiest prattle, it often moved me to
tears,

Hers was the gratefullest heart I have found in a
child of her years—

Nay you remember our Emmie; you used to send her
the flowers;

How she would smile at 'em, play with 'em, talk to
'em hours after hours !

They that can wander at will where the works of the
Lord are reveal'd

Little guess what joy can be got from a cowslip out
of the field ;

Flowers to these ' spirits in prison ' are all they can
know of the spring,

They freshen and sweeten the wards like the waft of
an Angel's wing ;

And she lay with a flower in one hand and her thin
hands crost on her breast—

Wan, but as pretty as heart can desire, and we thought
her at rest,

Quietly sleeping—so quiet, our doctor said 'Poor little
dear,

Nurse, I must do it to-morrow; she'll never live thro'
it, I fear.'

V.

I walk'd with our kindly old Doctor as far as the
head of the stair,

Then I return'd to the ward; the child didn't see I
was there.

VI.

Never since I was nurse, had I been so grieved and
so vext!

Emmie had heard him.   Softly she call'd from her cot
to the next,

'He says I shall never live thro' it, O Annie, what
    shall I do ? '

Annie consider'd. 'If I,' said the wise little Annie,
    ' was you,

I should cry to the dear Lord Jesus to help me, for,
    Emmie, you see,

It's all in the picture there : " Little children should
    come to me." '

(Meaning the print that you gave us, I find that it
    always can please

Our children, the dear Lord Jesus with children about
    his knees.)

'Yes, and I will,' said Emmie, ' but then if I call to
    the Lord,

How should he know that it's me ? such a lot of beds
    in the ward ! '

That was a puzzle for Annie. Again she consider'd
    and said :

' Emmie, you put out your arms, and you leave 'em

outside on the bed—

The Lord has so *much* to see to ! but, Emmie, you tell

it him plain,

It's the little girl with her arms lying out on the

counterpane.'

VII.

I had sat three nights by the child—I could not watch

her for four—

My brain had begun to reel—I felt I could do it no

more.

That was my sleeping-night, but I thought that it

never would pass.

There was a thunderclap once, and a clatter of hail on

the glass,

And there was a phantom cry that I heard as I tost about,

The motherless bleat of a lamb in the storm and the darkness without;

My sleep was broken besides with dreams of the dreadful knife

And fears for our delicate Emmie who scarce would escape with her life;

Then in the gray of the morning it seem'd she stood by me and smiled,

And the doctor came at his hour, and we went to see to the child.

VIII.

He had brought his ghastly tools: we believed her asleep again—

Her dear, long, lean, little arms lying out on the counterpane;

Say that His day is done!   Ah why should we care

 what they say?

The Lord of the children had heard her, and Emmie

 had past away.

DEDICATORY POEM TO THE
PRINCESS ALICE.

DEAD PRINCESS, living Power, if that, which lived

True life, live on—and if the fatal kiss,

Born of true life and love, divorce thee not

From earthly love and life—if what we call

The spirit flash not all at once from out

This shadow into Substance—then perhaps

The mellow'd murmur of the people's praise

From thine own State, and all our breadth of realm,

Where Love and Longing dress thy deeds in light,

Ascends to thee; and this March morn that sees

Thy Soldier-brother's bridal orange-bloom

Break thro' the yews and cypress of thy grave,

H

And thine Imperial mother smile again,

May send one ray to thee ! and who can tell—

Thou—England's England-loving daughter—thou

Dying so English thou wouldst have her flag

Borne on thy coffin—where is he can swear

But that some broken gleam from our poor earth

May touch thee, while remembering thee, I lay

At thy pale feet this ballad of the deeds

Of England, and her banner in the East ?

THE DEFENCE OF LUCKNOW.

I.

BANNER of England, not for a season, O banner of
Britain, hast thou

Floated in conquering battle or flapt to the battle-
cry !

Never with mightier glory than when we had rear'd
thee on high

Flying at top of the roofs in the ghastly siege of
Lucknow—

Shot thro' the staff or the halyard, but ever we raised
thee anew,

And ever upon the topmost roof our banner of
England blew.

II

Frail were the works that defended the hold that we
held with our lives—

Women and children among us, God help them, our
children and wives !

Hold it we might—and for fifteen days or for twenty
at most.

'Never surrender, I charge you, but every man die at
his post ! '

Voice of the dead whom we loved, our Lawrence the
best of the brave :

Cold were his brows when we kiss'd him—we laid
him that night in his grave.

'Every man die at his post ! ' and there hail'd on our
houses and halls

Death from their rifle-bullets, and death from their
cannon-balls,

Death in our innermost chamber, and death at our
　　slight barricade,

Death while we stood with the musket, and death
　　while we stoopt to the spade,

Death to the dying, and wounds to the wounded, for
　　often there fell

Striking the hospital wall, crashing thro' it, their shot
　　and their shell,

Death—for their spies were among us, their marks-
　　men were told of our best,

So that the brute bullet broke thro' the brain that
　　could think for the rest ;

Bullets would sing by our foreheads, and bullets
　　would rain at our feet—

Fire from ten thousand at once of the rebels that
　　girdled us round—

Death at the glimpse of a finger from over the breadth
　　of a street,

Death from the heights of the mosque and the palace,
and death in the ground !

Mine ? yes, a mine ! Countermine ! down, down ! and
creep thro' the hole !

Keep the revolver in hand ! you can hear him—the
murderous mole !

Quiet, ah ! quiet—wait till the point of the pickaxe be
thro' !

Click with the pick, coming nearer and nearer again
than before—

Now let it speak, and you fire, and the dark pioneer is
no more ;

And ever upon the topmost roof our banner of England blew !

III.

Ay, but the foe sprung his mine many times, and it
    chanced on a day

Soon as the blast of that underground thunderclap
    echo'd away,

Dark thro' the smoke and the sulphur like so many
    fiends in their hell—

Cannon-shot, musket-shot, volley on volley, and yell
    upon yell—

Fiercely on all the defences our myriad enemy fell.

What have they done? where is it?   Out yonder.
    Guard the Redan !

Storm at the Water-gate ! storm at the Bailey-gate !
    storm, and it ran

Surging and swaying all round us, as ocean on every side

Plunges and heaves at a bank that is daily drown'd
    by the tide—

So many thousands that if they be bold enough, who
    shall escape ?

Kill or be kill'd, live or die, they shall know we are
    soldiers and men !

Ready ! take aim at their leaders—their masses are
    gapp'd with our grape—

Backward they reel like the wave, like the wave
    flinging forward again,

Flying and foil'd at the last by the handful they
    could not subdue ;

And ever upon the topmost roof our banner of Eng-
    land blew.

IV.

Handful of men as we were, we were English in
    heart and in limb,

Strong with the strength of the race to command, to
    obey, to endure,

Each of us fought as if hope for the garrison hung
but on him;

Still—could we watch at all points? we were every
day fewer and fewer.

There was a whisper among us, but only a whisper
that past:

'Children and wives—if the tigers leap into the fold
unawares—

Every man die at his post—and the foe may outlive
us at last—

Better to fall by the hands that they love, than to fall
into theirs!'

Roar upon roar in a moment two mines by the enemy
sprung

Clove into perilous chasms our walls and our poor
palisades.

Rifleman, true is your heart, but be sure that your
hand be as true!

Sharp is the fire of assault, better aimed are your
flank fusillades—

Twice do we hurl them to earth from the ladders to
which they had clung,

Twice from the ditch where they shelter we drive
them with hand-grenades;

And ever upon the topmost roof our banner of England blew.

V.

Then on another wild morning another wild earthquake out-tore

Clean from our lines of defence ten or twelve good
paces or more.

Rifleman, high on the roof, hidden there from the
light of the sun—

One has leapt up on the breach, crying out: 'Follow
me, follow me!'—

Mark him—he falls! then another, and *him* too, and

    down goes he.

Had they been bold enough then, who can tell but

    the traitors had won?

Boardings and rafters and doors — an embrasure!

    make way for the gun!

Now double-charge it with grape! It is charged and

    we fire, and they run.

Praise to our Indian brothers, and let the dark face

    have his due!

Thanks to the kindly dark faces who fought with us,

    faithful and few,

Fought with the bravest among us, and drove them,

    and smote them, and slew,

That ever upon the topmost roof our banner in India

    blew.

VI.

Men will forget what we suffer and not what we do.
We can fight

But to be soldier all day and be sentinel all thro'
the night—

Ever the mine and assault, our sallies, their lying
alarms.

Bugles and drums in the darkness, and shoutings and
soundings to arms,

Ever the labour of fifty that had to be done by five,

Ever the marvel among us that one should be left alive,

Ever the day with its traitorous death from the loop-
holes around,

Ever the night with its coffinless corpse to be laid in
the ground,

Heat like the mouth of a hell, or a deluge of cataract
skies,

Stench of old offal decaying, and infinite torment of
flies,

Thoughts of the breezes of May blowing over an
English field

Cholera, scurvy, and fever, the wound that *would* not
be heal'd,

Lopping away of the limb by the pitiful-pitiless
knife,—

Torture and trouble in vain,—for it never could save
us a life.

Valour of delicate women who tended the hospital
bed,

Horror of women in travail among the dying and
dead,

Grief for our perishing children, and never a moment
for grief,

Toil and ineffable weariness, faltering hopes of relief,

Havelock baffled, or beaten, or butcher'd for all that
we knew—

Then day and night, day and night, coming down on
    the still-shatter'd walls

Millions of musket-bullets, and thousands of cannon-
    balls—

But ever upon the topmost roof our banner of England
    blew

VII.

Hark cannonade, fusillade ! is it true what was told
    by the scout,

Outram and Havelock breaking their way through
    the fell mutineers ?

Surely the pibroch of Europe is ringing again in our
    ears !

All on a sudden the garrison utter a jubilant shout,

Havelock's glorious Highlanders answer with con-
    quering cheers,

Sick from the hospital echo them, women and children
    come out,

Blessing the wholesome white faces of Havelock's
good fusileers,

Kissing the war-harden'd hand of the Highlander wet
with their tears !

Dance to the pibroch !—saved ! we are saved !—is it
you ? is it you ?

Saved by the valour of Havelock, saved by the blessing of Heaven !

' Hold it for fifteen days ! ' we have held it for eighty-
seven !

And ever aloft on the palace roof the old banner of
England blew.

SIR JOHN OLDCASTLE, LORD COBHAM.

(IN WALES.)

My friend should meet me somewhere hereabout
To take me to that hiding in the hills.

    I have broke their cage, no gilded one, I trow—
I read no more the prisoner's mute wail
Scribbled or carved upon the pitiless stone ;
I find hard rocks, hard life, hard cheer, or none,
For I am emptier than a friar's brains ;
But God is with me in this wilderness,
These wet black passes and foam-churning chasms,—
And God's free air, and hope of better things.

I would I knew their speech ; not now to glean,

Not now—I hope to do it—some scatter'd ears,

Some ears for Christ in this wild field of Wales—

But, bread, merely for bread.   This tongue that wagg'd

They said with such heretical arrogance

Against the proud archbishop Arundel—

So much God's cause was fluent in it—is here

But as a Latin Bible to the crowd ;

' Bara ! '—what use ?   The Shepherd, when I speak,

Vailing a sullen eyelid with his hard

' Dim Saesneg ' passes, wroth at things of old—

No fault of mine.   Had he God's word in Welsh

He might be kindlier : happily come the day !

Not least art thou, thou little Bethlehem

In Judah, for in thee the Lord was born ;

Nor thou in Britain, little Lutterworth,

Least, for in thee the word was born again.

I

Heaven-sweet Evangel, ever-living word,

Who whilome spakest to the South in Greek

About the soft Mediterranean shores,

And then in Latin to the Latin crowd,

As good need was—thou hast come to talk our isle.

Hereafter thou, fulfilling Pentecost,

Must learn to use the tongues of all the world.

Yet art thou thine own witness that thou bringest

Not peace, a sword, a fire.

     What did he say,

My frighted Wiclif-preacher whom I crost

In flying hither? that one night a crowd

Throng'd the waste field about the city gates:

The king was on them suddenly with a host.

Why there? they came to hear their preacher.   Then

Some cried on Cobham, on the good Lord Cobham;

Ay, for they love me! but the king—nor voice

Nor finger raised against him—took and hang'd,

Took, hang'd and burnt—how many—thirty-nine—

Call'd it rebellion—hang'd, poor friends, as rebels

And burn'd alive as heretics! for your Priest

Labels—to take the king along with him—

All heresy, treason: but to call men traitors

May make men traitors.

                         Rose of Lancaster,

Red in thy birth, redder with household war,

Now reddest with the blood of holy men,

Redder to be, red rose of Lancaster—

If somewhere in the North, as Rumour sang

Fluttering the hawks of this crown-lusting line—

By firth and loch thy silver sister grow,[1]

That were my rose, there my allegiance due.

Self-starved, they say—nay, murder'd doubtless dead.

So to this king I cleaved: my friend was he,

Once my fast friend: I would have given my life

---

[1] Richard II.

To help his own from scathe, a thousand lives

To save his soul.   He might have come to learn

Our Wiclif's learning : but the worldly Priests

Who fear the king's hard common-sense should find

What rotten piles uphold their masonwork,

Urge him to foreign war.   O had he will'd

I might have stricken a lusty stroke for him,

But he would not ; far liever led my friend

Back to the pure and universal church,

But he would not : whether that heirless flaw

In his throne's title make him feel so frail,

He leans on Antichrist ; or that his mind,

So quick, so capable in soldiership,

In matters of the faith, alas the while !

More worth than all the kingdoms of this world,

Runs in the rut, a coward to the Priest.

Burnt—good Sir Roger Acton, my dear friend !

Burnt too, my faithful preacher, Beverley !

Lord give thou power to thy two witnesses !

Lest the false faith make merry over them !

Two—nay but thirty-nine have risen and stand,

Dark with the smoke of human sacrifice,

Before thy light, and cry continually—

Cry—against whom ?

               Him, who should bear the sword

Of Justice—what ! the kingly, kindly boy ;

Who took the world so easily heretofore,

My boon companion, tavern-fellow—him

Who gibed and japed—in many a merry tale

That shook our sides—at Pardoners, Summoners,

Friars, absolution-sellers, monkeries

And nunneries, when the wild hour and the wine

Had set the wits aflame.

                              Harry of Monmouth,

Or Amurath of the East ?

                              Better to sink

Thy fleurs-de-lys in slime again, and fling

Thy royalty back into the riotous fits

Of wine and harlotry—thy shame, and mine,

Thy comrade—than to persecute the Lord,

And play the Saul that never will be Paul.

        Burnt, burnt ! and while this mitred Arundel

Dooms our unlicensed preacher to the flame,

The mitre-sanction'd harlot draws his clerks

Into the suburb—their hard celibacy,

Sworn to be veriest ice of pureness, molten

Into adulterous living, or such crimes

As holy Paul—a shame to speak of them—

Among the heathen—

                              Sanctuary granted

To bandit, thief, assassin—yea to him

Who hacks his mother's throat—denied to him,

Who finds the Saviour in his mother tongue.

The Gospel, the Priest's pearl, flung down to swine—

The swine, lay-men, lay-women, who will come,

God willing, to outlearn the filthy friar.

Ah rather, Lord, than that thy Gospel, meant

To course and range thro' all the world, should be

Tether'd to these dead pillars of the Church—

Rather than so, if thou wilt have it so,

Burst vein, snap sinew, and crack heart, and life

Pass in the fire of Babylon ! but how long,

O Lord, how long !

          My friend should meet me here.

Here is the copse, the fountain and—a Cross !

To thee, dead wood, I bow not head nor knees.

Rather to thee, green boscage, work of God,

Black holly, and white-flower'd wayfaring-tree !

Rather to thee, thou living water, drawn

By this good Wiclif mountain down from heaven,

And speaking clearly in thy native tongue—

No Latin—He that thirsteth, come and drink !

Eh ! how I anger'd Arundel asking me

To worship Holy Cross !   I spread mine arms,

God's work, I said, a cross of flesh and blood

And holier.   That was heresy.   (My good friend

By this time should be with me.)   'Images ?'

'Bury them as God's truer images

Are daily buried.'   'Heresy.—Penance ?'   'Fast,

Hairshirt and scourge—nay, let a man repent,

Do penance in his heart, God hears him.'   'Heresy—

Not shriven, not saved ?'   'What profits an ill Priest

Between me and my God ?   I would not spurn

Good counsel of good friends, but shrive myself

No, not to an Apostle.'   'Heresy.'

(My friend is long in coming.)   'Pilgrimages?'

'Drink, bagpipes, revelling, devil's-dances, vice.

The poor man's money gone to fat the friar.

Who reads of begging saints in Scripture?'—'Heresy'—

(Hath he been here—not found me—gone again?

Have I mislearnt our place of meeting?)   'Bread—

Bread left after the blessing?' how they stared,

That was their main test-question—glared at me!

'He veil'd Himself in flesh, and now He veils

His flesh in bread, body and bread together.'

Then rose the howl of all the cassock'd wolves,

'No bread, no bread.   God's body!'   Archbishop,

     Bishop,

Priors, Canons, Friars, bellringers, Parish-clerks—

'No bread, no bread!'—'Authority of the Church,

Power of the keys!'—Then I, God help me, I

So mock'd, so spurn'd, so baited two whole days—

I lost myself and fell from evenness,

And rail'd at all the Popes, that ever since

Sylvester shed the venom of world-wealth

Into the church, had only prov'n themselves

Poisoners, murderers.   Well—God pardon all—

Me, them, and all the world—yea, that proud Priest,

That mock-meek mouth of utter Antichrist,

That traitor to King Richard and the truth,

Who rose and doom'd me to the fire.

                                     Amen !

Nay, I can burn, so that the Lord of life

Be by me in my death.

                            Those three ! the fourth

Was like the son of God.   Not burnt were they.

On *them* the smell of burning had not past.

That was a miracle to convert the king.

These Pharisees, this Caiaphas-Arundel

What miracle could turn ?   *He* here again,

He thwarting their traditions of Himself,

He would be found a heretic to Himself,

And doom'd to burn alive.

　　　　　　　　So, caught, I burn.

Burn? heathen men have borne as much as this,

For freedom, or the sake of those they loved,

Or some less cause, some cause far less than mine;

For every other cause is less than mine.

The moth will singe her wings, and singed return,

Her love of light quenching her fear of pain—

How now, my soul, we do not heed the fire?

Faint-hearted? tut!—faint-stomach'd! faint as I am,

God willing, I will burn for Him.

　　　　　　　　Who comes?

A thousand marks are set upon my head.

Friend?—foe perhaps—a tussle for it then!

Nay, but my friend. Thou art so well disguised,

I knew thee not. Hast thou brought bread with thee?

I have not broken bread for fifty hours.

None ?   I am damn'd already by the Priest

For holding there was bread where bread was none—

No bread.   My friends await me yonder ?   Yes.

Lead on then.   *Up* the mountain ?   Is it far ?

Not far.   Climb first and reach me down thy hand.

I am not like to die for lack of bread,

For I must live to testify by fire.[1]

---

[1] He was burnt on Christmas Day, 1417.

COLUMBUS.

CHAINS, my good lord : in your raised brows I read

Some wonder at our chamber ornaments.

We brought this iron from our isles of gold.

Does the king know you deign to visit him

Whom once he rose from off his throne to greet

Before his people, like his brother king ?

I saw your face that morning in the crowd.

At Barcelona—tho' you were not then

So bearded.   Yes.   The city deck'd herself

To meet me, roar'd my name ; the king, the queen

Bad me be seated, speak, and tell them all

The story of my voyage, and while I spoke

The crowd's roar fell as at the ' Peace, be still ! '

And when I ceased to speak, the king, the queen,

Sank from their thrones, and melted into tears,

And knelt, and lifted hand and heart and voice

In praise to God who led me thro' the waste.

And then the great ' Laudamus ' rose to heaven.

Chains for the Admiral of the Ocean ! chains

For him who gave a new heaven, a new earth,

As holy John had prophesied of me,

Gave glory and more empire to the kings

Of Spain than all their battles ! chains for him

Who push'd his prows into the setting sun,

And made West East, and sail'd the Dragon's mouth,

And came upon the Mountain of the World,

And saw the rivers roll from Paradise !

Chains ! we are Admirals of the Ocean, we,

We and our sons for ever.   Ferdinand

Hath sign'd it and our Holy Catholic queen—

Of the Ocean—of the Indies—Admirals we—

Our title, which we never mean to yield,

Our guerdon not alone for what we did,

But our amends for all we might have done—

The vast occasion of our stronger life—

Eighteen long years of waste, seven in your Spain,

Lost, showing courts and kings a truth the babe

Will suck in with his milk hereafter—earth

A sphere.

Were *you* at Salamanca ?   No.

We fronted there the learning of all Spain,

All their cosmogonies, their astronomies :

Guess-work *they* guess'd it, but the golden guess

Is morning-star to the full round of truth.

No guess-work ! I was certain of my goal ;

Some thought it heresy, but that would not hold.

King David call'd the heavens a hide, a tent

Spread over earth, and so this earth was flat :

Some cited old Lactantius : could it be

That trees grew downward, rain fell upward, men

Walk'd like the fly on ceilings ? and besides,

The great Augustine wrote that none could breathe

Within the zone of heat ; so might there be

Two Adams, two mankinds, and that was clean

Against God's word : thus was I beaten back,

And chiefly to my sorrow by the Church,

And thought to turn my face from Spain, appeal

Once more to France or England ; but our Queen

Recall'd me, for at last their Highnesses

Were half-assured this earth might be a sphere.

All glory to the all-blessed Trinity,

All glory to the mother of our Lord,

And Holy Church, from whom I never swerved

Not even by one hair's-breadth of heresy,

I have accomplish'd what I came to do.

Not yet—not all—last night a dream—I sail'd

On my first voyage, harass'd by the frights

Of my first crew, their curses and their groans.

The great flame-banner borne by Teneriffe,

The compass, like an old friend false at last

In our most need, appall'd them, and the wind

Still westward, and the weedy seas—at length

The landbird, and the branch with berries on it,

The carven staff—and last the light, the light

On Guanahani! but I changed the name;

San Salvador I call'd it; and the light

Grew as I gazed, and brought out a broad sky

Of dawning over—not those alien palms,

The marvel of that fair new nature—not

That Indian isle, but our most ancient East

Moriah with Jerusalem ; and I saw

The glory of the Lord flash up, and beat

Thro' all the homely town from jasper, sapphire,

Chalcedony, emerald, sardonyx, sardius,

Chrysolite, beryl, topaz, chrysoprase,

Jacynth, and amethyst—and those twelve gates,

Pearl—and I woke, and thought—death—I shall die—

I am written in the Lamb's own Book of Life

To walk within the glory of the Lord

Sunless and moonless, utter light—but no !

The Lord had sent this bright, strange dream to me

To mind me of the secret vow I made

When Spain was waging war against the Moor—

I strove myself with Spain against the Moor.

There came two voices from the Sepulchre,

Two friars crying that if Spain should oust

The Moslem from her limit, he, the fierce

Soldan of Egypt, would break down and raze

The blessed tomb of Christ; whereon I vow'd

That, if our Princes harken'd to my prayer,

Whatever wealth I brought from that new world

Should, in this old, be consecrate to lead

A new crusade against the Saracen,

And free the Holy Sepulchre from thrall.

Gold? I had brought your Princes gold enough

If left alone! Being but a Genovese,

I am handled worse than had I been a Moor,

And breach'd the belting wall of Cambalu,

And given the Great Khan's palaces to the Moor,

Or clutch'd the sacred crown of Prester John,

And cast it to the Moor : but *had* I brought

From Solomon's now-recover'd Ophir all

The gold that Solomon's navies carried home,

Would that have gilded *me* ? Blue blood of Spain,

Tho' quartering your own royal arms of Spain,

I have not : blue blood and black blood of Spain,

The noble and the convict of Castile,

Howl'd me from Hispaniola ; for you know

The flies at home, that ever swarm about

And cloud the highest heads, and murmur down

Truth in the distance—these outbuzz'd me so

That even our prudent king, our righteous queen—

I pray'd them being so calumniated

They would commission one of weight and worth

To judge between my slander'd self and me—

Fonseca my main enemy at their court,

They send me out *his* tool, Bovadilla, one

As ignorant and impolitic as a beast—

Blockish irreverence, brainless greed—who sack'd

My dwelling, seized upon my papers, loosed

My captives, feed the rebels of the crown,

Sold the crown-farms for all but nothing, gave

All but free leave for all to work the mines,

Drove me and my good brothers home in chains,

And gathering ruthless gold—a single piece

Weigh'd nigh four thousand Castillanos—so

They tell me—weigh'd him down into the abysm—

The hurricane of the latitude on him fell,

The seas of our discovering over-roll

Him and his gold; the frailer caravel,

With what was mine, came happily to the shore.

There was a glimmering of God's hand.

                                And God

Hath more than glimmer'd on me.   O my lord,

I swear to you I heard his voice between

The thunders in the black Veragua nights,

'O soul of little faith, slow to believe !

Have I not been about thee from thy birth ?

Given thee the keys of the great Ocean-sea ?

Set thee in light till time shall be no more ?

Is it I who have deceived thee or the world ?

Endure ! thou hast done so well for men, that men

Cry out against thee : was it otherwise

With mine own Son ? '

                                And more than once in days

Of doubt and cloud and storm, when drowning hope

Sank all but out of sight, I heard his voice,

' Be not cast down.   I lead thee by the hand,

Fear not.'   And I shall hear his voice again—

I know that he has led me all my life,

I am not yet too old to work his will—

His voice again.

                        Still for all that, my lord,

I lying here bedridden and alone,

Cast off, put by, scouted by court and king—

The first discoverer starves—his followers, all

Flower into fortune—our world's way—and I,

Without a roof that I can call mine own,

With scarce a coin to buy a meal withal,

And seeing what a door for scoundrel scum

I open'd to the West, thro' which the lust,

Villany, violence, avarice, of your Spain

Pour'd in on all those happy naked isles—

Their kindly native princes slain or slaved,

Their wives and children Spanish concubines,

Their innocent hospitalities quench'd in blood,

Some dead of hunger, some beneath the scourge,

Some over-labour'd, some by their own hands,—

Yea, the dear mothers, crazing Nature, kill

Their babies at the breast for hate of Spain—

Ah God, the harmless people whom we found

In Hispaniola's island-Paradise !

Who took us for the very Gods from Heaven,

And we have sent them very fiends from Hell ;

And I myself, myself not blameless, I

Could sometimes wish I had never led the way.

Only the ghost of our great Catholic Queen

Smiles on me, saying, ' Be thou comforted !

This creedless people will be brought to Christ

And own the holy governance of Rome.'

But who could dream that we, who bore the Cross

Thither, were excommunicated there,

For curbing crimes that scandalised the Cross,

By him, the Catalonian Minorite,

Rome's Vicar in our Indies ? who believe

These hard memorials of our truth to Spain

Clung closer to us for a longer term

Than any friend of ours at Court? and yet

Pardon—too harsh, unjust.   I am rack'd with pains.

You see that I have hung them by my bed,

And I will have them buried in my grave.

Sir, in that flight of ages which are God's

Own voice to justify the dead—perchance

Spain once the most chivalric race on earth,

Spain then the mightiest, wealthiest realm on earth,

So made by me, may seek to unbury me,

To lay me in some shrine of this old Spain,

Or in that vaster Spain I leave to Spain.

Then some one standing by my grave will say,

'Behold the bones of Christopher Colòn'—

'Ay, but the chains, what do *they* mean—the

    chains?'—

I sorrow for that kindly child of Spain

Who then will have to answer, ' These same chains

Bound these same bones back thro' the Atlantic sea,

Which he unchain'd for all the world to come.'

O Queen of Heaven who seest the souls in Hell

And purgatory, I suffer all as much

As they do—for the moment.   Stay, my son

Is here anon: my son will speak for me

Ablier than I can in these spasms that grind

Bone against bone.   You will not.   One last word.

You move about the Court, I pray you tell

King Ferdinand who plays with me, that one,

Whose life has been no play with him and his

Hidalgos—shipwrecks, famines, fevers, fights,

Mutinies, treacheries—wink'd at, and condoned—

That I am loyal to him till the death,

And ready—tho' our Holy Catholic Queen,

Who fain had pledged her jewels on my first voyage,

Whose hope was mine to spread the Catholic faith,

Who wept with me when I return'd in chains,

Who sits beside the blessed Virgin now,

To whom I send my prayer by night and day—

She is gone—but you will tell the King, that I,

Rack'd as I am with gout, and wrench'd with pains

Gain'd in the service of His Highness, yet

Am ready to sail forth on one last voyage,

And readier, if the King would hear, to lead

One last crusade against the Saracen,

And save the Holy Sepulchre from thrall.

Going? I am old and slighted: you have dared

Somewhat perhaps in coming? my poor thanks!

I am but an alien and a Genovese.

THE VOYAGE OF MAELDUNE.

(FOUNDED ON AN IRISH LEGEND.   A.D. 700.)

I.

I WAS the chief of the race—he had stricken my father dead—

But I gather'd my fellows together, I swore I would strike off his head.

Each of them look'd like a king, and was noble in birth as in worth,

And each of them boasted he sprang from the oldest race upon earth.

Each was as brave in the fight as the bravest hero of song,

And each of them liefer had died than have done one another a wrong.

He lived on an isle in the ocean—we sail'd on a
Friday morn—

He that had slain my father the day before I was
born.

II.

And we came to the isle in the ocean, and there on
the shore was he.

But a sudden blast blew us out and away thro' a
boundless sea.

III.

And we came to the Silent Isle that we never had
touch'd at before,

Where a silent ocean always broke on a silent shore,

And the brooks glitter'd on in the light without
sound, and the long waterfalls

Pour'd in a thunderless plunge to the base of the
mountain walls,

And the poplar and cypress unshaken by storm

> flourish'd up beyond sight,

And the pine shot aloft from the crag to an un-

> believable height,

And high in the heaven above it there flicker'd a

> songless lark,

And the cock couldn't crow, and the bull couldn't

> low, and the dog couldn't bark.

And round it we went, and thro' it, but never a

> murmur, a breath—

It was all of it fair as life, it was all of it quiet as death,

And we hated the beautiful Isle, for whenever we

> strove to speak

Our voices were thinner and fainter than any flitter-

> mouse-shriek ;

And the men that were mighty of tongue and could

> raise such a battle-cry

That a hundred who heard it would rush on a

> thousand lances and die—

O they to be dumb'd by the charm!—so fluster'd
with anger were they

They almost fell on each other; but after we sail'd
away.

IV.

And we came to the Isle of Shouting, we landed, a
score of wild birds

Cried from the topmost summit with human voices
and words;

Once in an hour they cried, and whenever their
voices peal'd

The steer fell down at the plow and the harvest
died from the field,

And the men dropt dead in the valleys and half of
the cattle went lame,

And the roof sank in on the hearth, and the dwelling
broke into flame;

And the shouting of these wild birds ran into the
hearts of my crew,

Till they shouted along with the shouting and seized
one another and slew;

But I drew them the one from the other; I saw that
we could not stay,

And we left the dead to the birds and we sail'd with
our wounded away.

v.

And we came to the Isle of Flowers: their breath met
us out on the seas,

For the Spring and the middle Summer sat each on
the lap of the breeze;

And the red passion-flower to the cliffs, and the dark
blue clematis, clung,

And starr'd with a myriad blossom the long con-
volvulus hung;

And the topmost spire of the mountain was lilies in
lieu of snow,

And the lilies like glaciers winded down, running out
below

Thro' the fire of the tulip and poppy, the blaze of
gorse, and the blush

Of millions of roses that sprang without leaf or a
thorn from the bush ;

And the whole isle-side flashing down from the peak
without ever a tree

Swept like a torrent of gems from the sky to the
blue of the sea ;

And we roll'd upon capes of crocus and vaunted our
kith and our kin,

And we wallow'd in beds of lilies, and chanted the
triumph of Finn,

Till each like a golden image was pollen'd from head
to feet

And each was as dry as a cricket, with thirst in the
middle-day heat.

Blossom and blossom, and promise of blossom, but
never a fruit !

And we hated the Flowering Isle, as we hated the isle
that was mute,

And we tore up the flowers by the million and flung
them in bight and bay,

And we left but a naked rock, and in anger we sail'd
away.

VI.

And we came to the Isle of Fruits : all round from
the cliffs and the capes,

Purple or amber, dangled a hundred fathom of
grapes,

And the warm melon lay like a little sun on the
tawny sand,

And the fig ran up from the beach and rioted over
the land,

And the mountain arose like a jewell'd throne thro'
the fragrant air,

Glowing with all-colour'd plums and with golden
masses of pear,

And the crimson and scarlet of berries that flamed
upon bine and vine,

But in every berry and fruit was the poisonous
pleasure of wine;

And the peak of the mountain was apples, the hugest
that ever were seen,

And they prest, as they grew, on each other, with
hardly a leaflet between,

And all of them redder than rosiest health or than
utterest shame,

And setting, when Even descended, the very sunset
aflame ;

And we stay'd three days, and we gorged and we
madden'd, till every one drew

His sword on his fellow to slay him, and ever they
struck and they slew ;

And myself, I had eaten but sparely, and fought till I
sunder'd the fray,

Then I bad them remember my father's death, and we
sail'd away.

VII.

And we came to the Isle of Fire : we were lured by
the light from afar,

For the peak sent up one league of fire to the
Northern Star ;

Lured by the glare and the blare, but scarcely could

    stand upright,

For the whole isle shudder'd and shook like a man in

    a mortal affright;

We were giddy besides with the fruits we had

    gorged, and so crazed that at last

There were some leap'd into the fire; and away we

    sail'd, and we past

Over that undersea isle, where the water is clearer

    than air :

Down we look'd : what a garden ! O bliss, what a

    Paradise there !

Towers of a happier time, low down in a rainbow deep

Silent palaces, quiet fields of eternal sleep !

And three of the gentlest and best of my people,

    whate'er I could say,

Plunged head down in the sea, and the Paradise

    trembled away.

VIII.

And we came to the Bounteous Isle, where the heavens lean low on the land,

And ever at dawn from the cloud glitter'd o'er us a sunbright hand,

Then it open'd and dropt at the side of each man, as he rose from his rest,

Bread enough for his need till the labourless day dipt under the West;

And we wander'd about it and thro' it.   O never was time so good !

And we sang of the triumphs of Finn, and the boast of our ancient blood,

And we gazed at the wandering wave as we sat by the gurgle of springs,

And we chanted the songs of the Bards and the glories of fairy kings;

But at length we began to be weary, to sigh, and to
stretch and yawn,

Till we hated the Bounteous Isle and the sunbright
hand of the dawn,

For there was not an enemy near, but the whole
green Isle was our own,

And we took to playing at ball, and we took to
throwing the stone,

And we took to playing at battle, but that was a
perilous play,

For the passion of battle was in us, we slew and we
sail'd away.

IX.

And we came to the Isle of Witches and heard their
musical cry—

'Come to us, O come, come' in the stormy red of a
sky

Dashing the fires and the shadows of dawn on the
beautiful shapes,

For a wild witch naked as heaven stood on each of the
loftiest capes,

And a hundred ranged on the rock like white sea-
birds in a row,

And a hundred gamboll'd and pranced on the wrecks
in the sand below,

And a hundred splash'd from the ledges, and bosom'd
the burst of the spray,

But I knew we should fall on each other, and hastily
sail'd away.

X.

And we came in an evil time to the Isle of the
Double Towers

One was of smooth-cut stone, one carved all over with
flowers

But an earthquake always moved in the hollows under
the dells,

And they shock'd on each other and butted each other
with clashing of bells,

And the daws flew out of the Towers and jangled and
wrangled in vain,

And the clash and boom of the bells rang into the
heart and the brain,

Till the passion of battle was on us, and all took sides
with the Towers,

There were some for the clean-cut stone, there were
more for the carven flowers,

And the wrathful thunder of God peal'd over us all
the day,

For the one half slew the other, and after we sail'd
away.

XI.

And we came to the Isle of a Saint who had sail'd

with St. Brendan of yore,

He had lived ever since on the Isle and his winters

were fifteen score,

And his voice was low as from other worlds, and his

eyes were sweet,

And his white hair sank to his heels and his white

beard fell to his feet,

And he spake to me, 'O Maeldune, let be this purpose

of thine!

Remember the words of the Lord when he told us

" Vengeance is mine!"

His fathers have slain thy fathers in war or in single

strife,

Thy fathers have slain his fathers, each taken a life

for a life,

Thy father had slain his father, how long shall the
    murder last ?

Go back to the Isle of Finn and suffer the Past to be
    Past.'

And we kiss'd the fringe of his beard and we pray'd
    as we heard him pray,

And the Holy man he assoil'd us, and sadly we sail'd
    away.

XII.

And we came to the Isle we were blown from, and
    there on the shore was he,

The man that had slain my father. I saw him and
    let him be.

O weary was I of the travel, the trouble, the strife
    and the sin,

When I landed again, with a tithe of my men, on the
    Isle of Finn.

DE PROFUNDIS.

THE TWO GREETINGS.

I.

OUT of the deep, my child, out of the deep,

Where all that was to be, in all that was,

Whirl'd for a million æons thro' the vast

Waste dawn of multitudinous-eddying light—

Out of the deep, my child, out of the deep,

Thro' all this changing world of changeless law,

And every phase of ever-heightening life,

And nine long months of antenatal gloom,

With this last moon, this crescent—her dark orb

Touch'd with earth's light—thou comest, darling

boy;

Our own; a babe in lineament and limb

Perfect, and prophet of the perfect man;

Whose face and form are hers and mine in one,

Indissolubly married like our love;

Live, and be happy in thyself, and serve

This mortal race thy kin so well, that men

May bless thee as we bless thee, O young life

Breaking with laughter from the dark; and may

The fated channel where thy motion lives

Be prosperously shaped, and sway thy course

Along the years of haste and random youth

Unshatter'd; then full-current thro' full man;

And last in kindly curves, with gentlest fall,

By quiet fields, a slowly-dying power,

To that last deep where we and thou are still.

I.

OUT of the deep, my child, out of the deep,

From that great deep, before our world begins,

Whereon the Spirit of God moves as he will—

Out of the deep, my child, out of the deep,

From that true world within the world we see,

Whereof our world is but the bounding shore—

Out of the deep, Spirit, out of the deep,

With this ninth moon, that sends the hidden sun

Down yon dark sea, thou comest, darling boy.

II.

For in the world, which is not ours, They said

' Let us make man' and that which should be man,

From that one light no man can look upon,

Drew to this shore lit by the suns and moons

And all the shadows. O dear Spirit half-lost

In thine own shadow and this fleshly sign

That thou art thou—who wailest being born

And banish'd into mystery, and the pain

Of this divisible-indivisible world,

Among the numerable-innumerable

Sun, sun, and sun, thro' finite-infinite space

In finite-infinite Time—our mortal veil

And shatter'd phantom of that infinite One,

Who made thee unconceivably Thyself

Out of His whole World-self and all in all—

Live thou ! and of the grain and husk, the grape

And ivyberry, choose ; and still depart

From death to death thro' life and life, and find

Nearer and ever nearer Him, who wrought

Not Matter, nor the finite-infinite,

But this main-miracle, that thou art thou,

With power on thine own act and on the world.

THE HUMAN CRY.

I.

HALLOWED be Thy name—Halleluiah!—

Infinite Ideality!

Immeasurable Reality!

Infinite Personality!

Hallowed be Thy name—Halleluiah!

II.

We feel we are nothing—for all is Thou and in Thee;

We feel we are something—*that* also has come from

Thee;

We know we are nothing—but Thou wilt help us

to be.

Hallowed be Thy name—Halleluiah!

M

PREFATORY SONNET

TO THE 'NINETEENTH CENTURY.'

THOSE that of late had fleeted far and fast

To touch all shores, now leaving to the skill

Of others their old craft seaworthy still,

Have charter'd this ; where, mindful of the past,

Our true co-mates regather round the mast ;

Of diverse tongue, but with a common will

Here, in this roaring moon of daffodil

And crocus, to put forth and brave the blast ;

For some, descending from the sacred peak

Of hoar high-templed Faith, have leagued again

Their lot with ours to rove the world about ;

And some are wilder comrades, sworn to seek

If any golden harbour be for men

In seas of Death and sunless gulfs of Doubt.

TO THE REV. W. H. BROOKFIELD.

Brooks, for they call'd you so that knew you best,

Old Brooks, who loved so well to mouth my rhymes,

How oft we two have heard St. Mary's chimes !

How oft the Cantab supper, host and guest,

Would echo helpless laughter to your jest !

How oft with him we paced that walk of limes,

Him, the lost light of those dawn-golden times,

Who loved you well !   Now both are gone to rest.

Yon man of humourous melancholy mark,

Dead of some inward agony—is it so ?

Our kindlier, trustier Jaques, past away !

I cannot laud this life, it looks so dark :

Σκιᾶς ὄναρ—dream of a shadow, go—

God bless you.   I shall join you in a day.

MONTENEGRO.

THEY rose to where their sovran eagle sails,

They kept their faith, their freedom, on the height,

Chaste, frugal, savage, arm'd by day and night

Against the Turk; whose inroad nowhere scales

Their headlong passes, but his footstep fails,

And red with blood the Crescent reels from fight

Before their dauntless hundreds, in prone fight

By thousands down the crags and thro' the vales.

O smallest among peoples! rough rock-throne

Of Freedom! warriors beating back the swarm

Of Turkish Islam for five hundred years,

Great Tsernogora! never since thine own

Black ridges drew the cloud and brake the storm

Has breathed a race of mightier mountaineers.

TO VICTOR HUGO.

VICTOR in Drama, Victor in Romance,

Cloud-weaver of phantasmal hopes and fears,

French of the French, and Lord of human tears;

Child-lover; Bard whose fame-lit laurels glance

Darkening the wreaths of all that would advance,

Beyond our strait, their claim to be thy peers;

Weird Titan by thy winter weight of years

As yet unbroken, Stormy voice of France!

Who dost not love our England—so they say;

I know not—England, France, all man to be

Will make one people ere man's race be run:

And I, desiring that diviner day,

Yield thee full thanks for thy full courtesy

To younger England in the boy my son.

TRANSLATIONS, ETC.

Constantinus, King of the Scots, after having sworn allegiance to Athelstan, allied himself with the Danes of Ireland
under Anlaf, and invading England, was defeated by Athelstan and his brother Edmund with great slaughter at
Brunanburh in the year 937.

I.

[1] ATHELSTAN King,

Lord among Earls,

Bracelet-bestower and

Baron of Barons,

He with his brother,

Edmund Atheling,

---

[1] I have more or less availed myself of my son's prose
translation of this poem in the *Contemporary Review* (No-
vember 1876).

Gaining a lifelong

Glory in battle,

Slew with the sword-edge

There by Brunanburh,

Brake the shield-wall,

Hew'd the lindenwood,[1]

Hack'd the battleshield,

Sons of Edward with hammer'd brands.

II.

Theirs was a greatness

Got from their Grandsires—

Theirs that so often in

Strife with their enemies

Struck for their hoards and their hearths and their

homes.

---

[1] Shields of lindenwood.

III.

Bow'd the spoiler,

Bent the Scotsman,

Fell the shipcrews

Doom'd to the death.

All the field with blood of the fighters

Flow'd, from when first the great

Sun-star of morningtide,

Lamp of the Lord God

Lord everlasting,

Glode over earth till the glorious creature

Sunk to his setting.

IV.

There lay many a man

Marr'd by the javelin,

Men of the Northland

Shot over shield.

There was the Scotsman

Weary of war.

v.

We the West-Saxons,

Long as the daylight

Lasted, in companies

Troubled the track of the host that we hated,

Grimly with swords that were sharp from the grind-

stone,

Fiercely we hack'd at the flyers before us.

vi.

Mighty the Mercian,

Hard was his hand-play,

Sparing not any of

Those that with Anlaf,

Warriors over the

Weltering waters

Borne in the bark's-bosom,

Drew to this island,

Doom'd to the death.

VII.

Five young kings put asleep by the sword-stroke,

Seven strong Earls of the army of Anlaf

Fell on the war-field, numberless numbers,

Shipmen and Scotsmen.

VIII.

Then the Norse leader,

Dire was his need of it,

Few were his following,

Fled to his warship :

Fleeted his vessel to sea with the king in it,

Saving his life on the fallow flood.

IX.

Also the crafty one,

Constantínus,

Crept to his·North again,

Hoar-headed hero !

X.

Slender reason had

He to be proud of

The welcome of war-knives—

He that was reft of his

Folk and his friends that had

Fallen in conflict,

Leaving his son too

Lost in the carnage,

Mangled to morsels,

A youngster in war !

XI.

Slender reason had

He to be glad of

The clash of the war-glaive—

Traitor and trickster

And spurner of treaties—

He nor had Anlaf

With armies so broken

A reason for bragging

That they had the better

In perils of battle

On places of slaughter—

The struggle of standards,

The rush of the javelins,

The crash of the charges,[1]

The wielding of weapons—

The play that they play'd with

The children of Edward.

XII.

Then with their nail'd prows

Parted the Norsemen, a

Blood-redden'd relic of

Javelins over

The jarring breaker, the deepsea billow,

Shaping their way toward Dyflen [2] again,

Shamed in their souls.

---

[1] Lit. 'the gathering of men.'   [2] Dublin.

XIII.

Also the brethren,

King and Atheling,

Each in his glory,

Went to his own in his own West-Saxonland,

Glad of the war.

XIV.

Many a carcase they left to be carrion,

Many a livid one, many a sallow-skin—

Left for the white-tail'd eagle to tear it, and

Left for the horny-nibb'd raven to rend it, and

Gave to the garbaging war-hawk to gorge it, and

That gray beast, the wolf of the weald.

N

XV.

Never had huger

Slaughter of heroes

Slain by the sword-edge—

Such as old writers

Have writ of in histories—

Hapt in this isle, since

Up from the East hither

Saxon and Angle from

Over the broad billow

Broke into Britain with

Haughty war-workers who

Harried the Welshman, when

Earls that were lured by the

Hunger of glory gat

Hold of the land.

ACHILLES OVER THE TRENCH.

ILIAD, xviii. 202.

So saying, light-foot Iris pass'd away.

Then rose Achilles dear to Zeus ; and round

The warrior's puissant shoulders Pallas flung

Her fringed ægis, and around his head

The glorious goddess wreath'd a golden cloud,

And from it lighted an all-shining flame.

As when a smoke from a city goes to heaven

Far off from out an island girt by foes,

All day the men contend in grievous war

From their own city, but with set of sun

Their fires flame thickly, and aloft the glare

Flies streaming, if perchance the neighbours round

May see, and sail to help them in the war;

So from his head the splendour went to heaven.

From wall to dyke he stept, he stood, nor join'd

The Achæans—honouring his wise mother's word—

There standing, shouted, and Pallas far away

Call'd; and a boundless panic shook the foe.

For like the clear voice when a trumpet shrills,

Blown by the fierce beleaguerers of a town,

So rang the clear voice of Æakidês;

And when the brazen cry of Æakidês

Was heard among the Trojans, all their hearts

Were troubled, and the full-maned horses whirl'd

The chariots backward, knowing griefs at hand;

And sheer-astounded were the charioteers

To see the dread, unweariable fire

That always o'er the great Peleion's head

Burn'd, for the bright-eyed goddess made it burn.

hrice from the dyke he sent his mighty shout,

hrice backward reel'd the Trojans and allies;

.nd there and then twelve of their noblest died

.mong their spears and chariots.

TO THE PRINCESS FREDERICA

ON HER MARRIAGE.

O you that were eyes and light to the King till he past

    away

    From the darkness of life—

He saw not his daughter—he blest her : the blind King

    sees you to-day,

    He blesses the wife.

SIR JOHN FRANKLIN.

ON THE CENOTAPH IN WESTMINSTER ABBEY.

NOT here ! the white North has thy bones ; and thou,

    Heroic sailor-soul,

Art passing on thine happier voyage now

    Toward no earthly pole.

TO DANTE.

(Written at request of the Florentines.)

King, that hast reign'd six hundred years, and grown

In power, and ever growest, since thine own

Fair Florence honouring thy nativity,

Thy Florence now the crown of Italy,

Hath sought the tribute of a verse from me,

I, wearing but the garland of a day,

Cast at thy feet one flower that fades away.

Spottiswcode and Co., Printers, New-street Square, London.

A LIST OF
THE VARIOUS FORMS IN WHICH
MR. TENNYSON'S WORKS
ARE PUBLISHED.

THE IMPERIAL LIBRARY EDITION OF THE COMPLETE WORKS,

In seven handsome demy octavo Volumes, printed in large clear old-faced type on toned paper, with a Steel Engraved Portrait of the Author, from a Photograph. Price £3. 13s. 6d. cloth ; or £4. 7s. 6d. Roxburgh. Each volume sold separately, price 10s. 6d. ; Roxburgh, half-morocco, 12s. 6d. each.

THE AUTHOR'S EDITION.

This Edition is in crown octavo, printed on superfine paper, with handsome margins, in clear old face type—each volume containing a Frontispiece. *This Edition can also be had bound in Roxburgh, half-morocco, price 1s. 6d. per vol. extra.*

THE MINIATURE EDITION,

In thirteen Volumes. Pocket size, bound in white or blue cloth extra, gilt leaves, in case, price 42s. *This Edition can also be had in plain binding and case, price 36s.*

THE GUINEA EDITION,

In Twelve volumes, neatly bound in cloth, and enclosed in box, price 21s. ; French morocco, price 31s. 6d.

THE ROYAL EDITION,

With Portrait and 25 Illustrations. In One Volume, cloth extra, bevelled boards, gilt leaves, price 21s.

THE CROWN EDITION,

In One Volume, cloth, price 6s. ; cloth extra, gilt leaves, price 7s. 6d. ; Roxburgh, half-morocco, price 8s. 6d.

THE SHILLING EDITION,

In Twelve Volumes (pocket size) sewed, price One Shilling each.

CONTENTS.

I.—Poems.
II.—Poems.
III.—Poems.
IV.—The Coming of Arthur ; Geraint and Enid ; Merlin and Vivian.
V.—Lancelot and Elaine ; The Holy Grail; Pelleas and Ettarre.
VI.—Guinevere ; Passing of Arthur ; Gareth and Lynette ; The Last Tournament.
VII.—In Memoriam.
VIII.—The Princess.
IX.—Maud, and other Poems.
X.—Enoch Arden.
XI.—Queen Mary.
XII.—Harold.

London : C. KEGAN PAUL & CO., 1 Paternoster Square.

THE CABINET EDITION.

This convenient and compact Edition is now complete. It consists of Twelve Volumes fcp. 8vo. printed in clear type, and bound in limp scarlet cloth. The first volume is illustrated with a beautiful Photographic Portrait of the Author, and each succeeding volume has a handsome Engraved Frontispiece. Price 2s. 6d. each volume.

CONTENTS OF THE VOLUMES.

Vol.   I.—**Early Poems.** Illustrated with a Photographic Portrait of Mr. Alfred Tennyson.

II.—**English Idylls,** and other Poems. Containing an Engraving of Mr. Alfred Tennyson's Residence at Aldworth.

III.—**Locksley Hall,** and other Poems. With an Engraved Picture of Farringford.

IV.—**Lucretius,** and other Poems. Containing an Engraving of a Scene in the Garden at Swainston.

V.—**Idylls of the King.** With an Autotype of the Bust of Mr. Alfred Tennyson by T. Woolner, R.A.

VI.—**Idylls of the King.** Illustrated with an Engraved Portrait of 'Elaine,' from a Photographic Study of Julia M. Cameron.

VII.—**Idylls of the King.** Containing an Engraving of 'Arthur,' from a Photographic Study of Julia M. Cameron.

VIII.—**The Princess.** With an Engraved Frontispiece of 'The Princess.'

IX.—**Maud,** and Enoch Arden. With a Portrait of 'Maud,' taken from a Photographic Study of Julia M. Cameron.

X.—**In Memoriam.** With a Steel Engraving of Arthur H. Hallam, engraved from a Picture in possession of the Author by J. C. Armytage.

XI.—**Queen Mary:** a Drama. With Engraved Frontispiece after Drawing by Walter Crane.

XII.—**Harold:** a Drama. With Engraved Frontispiece after Drawing by Walter Crane.

THE CABINET EDITION IN CASE.

This Edition is also issued in a handsome green case; forming an elegant ornament for the Drawing Room or Library Table.

PRICE, COMPLETE, THIRTY-TWO SHILLINGS.

London: C. KEGAN PAUL & CO., 1 Paternoster Square.